Land of Dreams

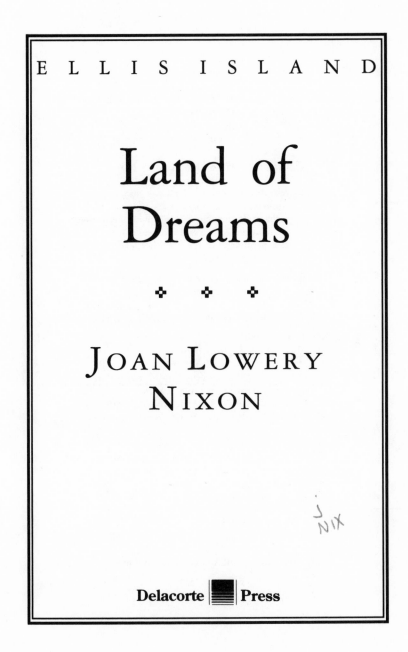

E L L I S   I S L A N D

Land of Dreams

JOAN LOWERY NIXON

Delacorte Press

Published by
Delacorte Press
Bantam Doubleday Dell Publishing Group, Inc.
1540 Broadway
New York, New York 10036

ᴡᴠ ᴡᴀ

Library of Congress Cataloging in Publication Data

Nixon, Joan Lowery.
    Land of dreams / by Joan Lowery Nixon.
        p.   cm.—(Ellis Island ; #3)
    Summary: In 1902 sixteen-year-old Kristin travels
with her family from Sweden to a new life in Minnesota,
where she finds herself frustrated by the restrictions
placed on what girls of her age are expected or allowed
to do.
    ISBN 0-385-31170-2
    [1. Swedish Americans—Fiction. 2. Emigration and
immigration—Fiction. 3. Minnesota—Fiction. 4. Sex
role—Fiction.]
    I. Title. II. Series: Nixon, Joan Lowery. Ellis Island ;
#3.
PZ7.N65Lal   1994
[Fic]—dc   93-8734   CIP   AC

Manufactured in the United States of America

February 1994

10   9   8   7   6   5   4   3   2   1

BVG

To Karen Nelson Hoyle,
curator of the Kerlan Collection,
Children's Literature Research Collection,
University of Minnesota,
in appreciation of her long dedication and devotion
to children's literature

CHAPTER ONE

❖ ❖ ❖

KRISTIN Swensen tossed her long blond braid over her shoulder and braced herself against the sides of the wagon. Its wheels thumped and jolted in the road's holes and ruts and Kristin could barely hear her father describing the land he had purchased.

"It has good, fertile soil," he told his wife, who sat beside him. "The property slopes down to the lake, and part of it is forested with pine, fir, oak, and maple. . . . I even saw some tamarack and ash—"

"Pappa," Kristin interrupted, "I want to hear about the house. You said there was already a house and barn on the property. Is it a real house? I mean, like our house in Sweden?"

Her father, perched high on the wooden wagon seat, twisted to look down at Kristin. He managed an impatient smile and said, "It's a simple two-story house, and it will be what we make of it. Now . . . will you allow me to tell this in my own way?"

Turning back to Kristin's mother, he said, "It's too late

1

in the season to plant an early wheat crop, and even a little late for corn, so our first crop will be summer potatoes. I've heard of a young man we can hire to help me prepare the ground for the potatoes and for your kitchen garden."

Kristin sighed impatiently. At the moment she wasn't interested in crops. She tried to picture the house, imagining the parlor with colorful *trasmattor* covering the gleaming, polished wood floor. She imagined chairs filled with pillows, their covers and throws woven of the brightest yarn. There'd be a loom in one corner, which Mamma would use during the long, bright summer evening hours before bedtime, and probably at the back of the house there would be a large indoor-outdoor pantry, much like the one they had in Sweden. She wondered if her bedroom would face the morning or the evening sun, and she wished for cool breezes to float through the open windows on summer nights.

Many people in the Great Rock Lake area of Minnesota had helped to welcome the newcomers, such as the shopkeepers, Oscar and Edla Lundgren, who had shared their living quarters above the store until the Swensens purchased land and a house. There'd been many new names and faces during the next few days—the Youngdahls, the Carlsons, the Stenborgs, the Berglunds, whose daughter Jenny was Kristin's age—and Kristin had noticed that each house they visited was decorated exactly as it would have been in Sweden. The food was the same. Even the language was the same. Pappa had insisted that his whole family learn to speak English before coming to the United States, yet so far everyone Kristin had met in the St. Croix Valley had spoken Swedish to her.

There was a lull in her parents' conversation. "While

we're together," Kristin suggested, "why don't we speak to each other in English? If we don't use the language, we'll forget what we've already learned."

Mamma put her hands to her face. "Later, Kristin," she said. "I can't concentrate in English, and there is too much in our new home to think about."

As they reached the top of a low hill, Pappa pointed ahead and to the left. "There it is," he said proudly. "There is our land."

A meadow, lush with green spring grass spread like a thick and lumpy blanket in its mounds and valleys, lay between the dirt road and a green forest beyond. Two thick planks bridged the fast-flowing stream that had carved a deep, twisting bed through the meadow.

"Where is the house?" Kristin asked eagerly.

Pappa laughed. "This parcel contains more land than I originally had in mind to buy. We'll soon come to the house."

The road curved and passed another uncleared clump of trees. Finally their new home stood before them.

Built of weathered raw lumber, the narrow house loomed two stories high over a tangle of scraggly weeds that must once have been a vegetable garden. The windows of the house were streaked and crusted with dirt; the summer kitchen squatted at one side like an old, tired troll. Remnants of a bird's nest hung from the top of the central chimney, and a few bricks had fallen from the chimney that poked through the roof of the summer kitchen.

"Well," Mamma said weakly. "Well. The house is very . . ." She clung to the wagon seat, unable to speak.

"It's ugly as a witch at midnight," Kristin said, "but at least it's a house." She hopped from the wagon and strode to the front door. "The door's unlocked," she called out, her hand on the knob. "Come, Mamma. Let's take a look inside."

Kristin's mouth opened with surprise as she stepped into the front room of the house, but she closed it quickly, batting a spiderweb away from her face. The room was furnished. Stained wooden chairs, their high backs against the walls, were grouped around an upholstered sofa. A table, protected from the oil lamp that centered it by a lacy crocheted runner, also held what looked like a family Bible and two small prayer books. The fireplace was large and deep, and next to it was tucked a cradle. But everything was covered with inches of dust and grime, and the lace curtains at the windows hung in rotted strips.

As Mamma stepped into the room beside her, Kristin took her hand and squeezed it. Trying to make her voice cheerful, she said a little too loudly, "Look! The house is furnished. Isn't it wonderful that we won't have to buy or build any furniture?"

Mamma studied the contents of the room. Then she asked, "Linnart, who lived in this house?"

Pappa joined them, stamping his feet as though he could shake loose the blanket of dust and make it disappear. "Why does it matter?" he replied with obvious discomfort.

"It matters," Mamma said stubbornly. She pointed toward the cradle. "There was a child—perhaps more than one. And look at the cloth in the loom—a woman was interrupted at her weaving. The people who lived here left suddenly without taking their possessions." Mamma's voice became sharper. "What happened to them?"

Pappa took a deep breath. Almost running his sentences together, he answered, "The wife and two children took ill with diphtheria and died. The husband had no more desire to remain. He turned the deed over to his cousin, who lives in Hay Lake, and left Minnesota. He never came back."

Mamma shivered and looked to each side. "There may be *spöken* in this house."

Kristin, well aware of her mother's belief in ghosts, moved a step closer to her. Every old castle in Sweden was supposed to be haunted by *spöken,* and this dusty, gloomy house also seemed a likely place. But her father answered firmly, "No, Gerda. There are no *spöken* here."

"We can't be sure."

Papa interrupted. "Sweden may be filled with ghosts, but we have left them behind. This country is too young to have ghosts." He smiled as he said, "We are more likely to have one of the little *tomtun* living here, protecting our house."

"A *tomte* will stay only if we remember to put out a bowl of rice pudding on Christmas Eve for it," Kristin said, glad for the change of subject. Even though many people in Sweden believed in *spöken,* long ago Kristin had tried to convince herself that there were no such things as ghosts. It was just that talk about them made her nervous. She walked past her parents to peer into the kitchen.

Pappa said, "Upstairs there are two large bedrooms and a room for storage. Would you like to see the rest of the house?"

Mamma glanced apprehensively toward the stairway. "I'll see it soon enough. We had better get to work. There's much to be done." She began to roll up her sleeves as she gave directions. "The curtains will have to be thrown out, and we'll get all the furniture out of the house and into the sunlight. A little oil rubbed into the wood will do wonders. That table—if you pick up one end, Linnart, and Kristin holds the other . . ."

"The beds are too large to carry down the stairs," Pappa told her. "They'd have to be taken apart."

"Then take them apart. And burn the mattresses and bedding." Mamma hesitated. "I'll make new mattresses. At the Lundgrens' general store I saw some heavy cotton ticking, and it should be easy enough to get straw to stuff the casings."

Kristin struggled to pick up one of the chairs, but her mother said, "Kristin! Get our things from the wagon. Put on your apron and kerchief before you do a single thing. Look at that dust! I saw a pump around back. See if it's working. If not, look for a rain barrel. Or take the bucket and bring water from the stream. We'll need lots of water and lye soap."

The Swensens worked hard, rarely stopping—except for occasional drinks of water—until noon, when Mamma unpacked the hamper Fru Lundgren had given them. They sat outside on the grass and ate thick slices of bread, wedges of creamy cheese, and apples.

Kristin unbuttoned the top two buttons on her high-necked dress and fanned herself with one hand. "It's so hot!" she complained.

Pappa nodded and said, "I was told the weather is unseasonable. It is quite warm for May, but it should cool down before long."

"I wish it would cool down this very minute," Kristin said, longing for Sweden's chilly weather. She stood up and squirmed as rivulets of sweat trickled down her back, making it itch.

As she picked up the bucket, Pappa said, "Take a few minutes to rest, Kristin. You've been working very hard."

"I'd like to finish. I've scrubbed every inch of the parlor, from ceiling to floor, and the kitchen comes next."

Mamma spoke up. "Your father is right. You've just eaten. You'll get a stitch in your side if you don't rest."

"It's too hot."

"Then go for a walk under the trees," Pappa told her. "If you follow that path, it will take you to the lake."

Kristin, eager to see more of their land, put down the bucket and headed for the forest.

It *was* much cooler under the trees. The path was overgrown in places, but Kristin easily made her way through the woods, stopping only when she reached Great Rock Lake, which was so large, the trees that bordered the far side were a dark green blur. Ducks paddled far out on the water, and the larger, web-footed loons dove for fish near wooded islands that broke the glittering expanse of blue. Close at hand Kristin saw a small, crescent-shaped beach, and beyond it a quiet pool.

On hot summer days in Sweden the local boys often threw off their clothes and splashed in the lake when no one else was around. Kristin always envied them this freedom. She laughed and looked around, then began to unbutton her dress. This secluded spot was hers alone. Now it was her turn to enjoy the cool water. There was no one to see her, no one to find out. She quickly stripped off her shoes and her dusty, sweat-stained clothing and flung herself into the water.

It was so cold, she yelped, trying to catch her breath, but as she rubbed her arms and legs, her body quickly grew used to the chill. She kicked and splashed, holding her nose and submerging, her loosened hair floating like a pale cloud above her. She was a magical water sprite; she was a fish. This was her own private pool, and she never wanted to leave it.

"Kristin! What are you doing?"

Startled, Kristin pushed aside her wet hair that was plastered over her eyes and looked toward the beach where Jenny Berglund stood watching, her blue eyes wide with astonishment, her hands pressed to her reddened cheeks.

Kristin had liked Jenny when she'd first met her at the Lundgrens' store. Jenny had a broad smile and the way the tip of her nose tilted upward, Kristin thought she looked like a wood sprite plotting mischief. Kristin had hoped they could be friends. Embarrassed at being caught, Kristin curled up tightly, keeping the water all the way to her chin, and tried to look nonchalant. "I'm cooling off in the lake," she said.

Jenny pointed at the heap of clothing lying on the ground. "But you . . . you have no clothes on."

"Clothes would get waterlogged and weigh me down. It's much nicer *without* clothes."

"It is?" Jenny's eyes met Kristin's with interest, and she took a step closer. "But what if someone should come along while you were . . . were . . . in this state of undress?"

"Someone just did," Kristin said, her discomfort increasing. "*You* did. You aren't going to tell, are you?"

"Never!" Jenny held a hand over her heart. "You're not like anyone else I've ever met. You're the most interesting person."

Kristin felt a surge of hope. Maybe Jenny would be a

good friend even though they just met. Kristin had a wonderful thing happen to her on the sea voyage to America; she'd become friends with Rose Carney and Rebekah Levinsky. From totally different cultures, Ireland and Russia, Rose and Rebekah had accepted Kristin for herself, and she in turn had appreciated their individuality. They weren't at all like the girls she had known in Sweden, who seemed to spend all their time learning to cook and bake and embroider, giggling together about the young men they'd someday marry and scorning Kristin, who was proud that she could beat any boy in town at fishing or riding bareback.

"Mark my words, Gerda, your Linnart has given that girl much too much freedom," Kristin had overheard her aunt, Hedvig, caution. "She's sixteen—close to seventeen—and in a year or two you won't find a father in Leksand who'll consider a match between your tomboy Kristin and his son."

"I know, I know. Linnart has recognized his mistake," Mamma had said, and Kristin flinched at the discouragement in her mother's voice. "From the time Kristin was very young, he let her work beside him and talked to her about farming and politics—all things he would have discussed with a son if he'd had one." Mamma had paused for just an instant, and when she spoke again, her words were filled with hope. "Maybe we can give Kristin a second chance at making a good marriage. Linnart has a dream of emigrating to the United States. Under socialism taxes are higher and higher in Sweden, and there is no longer great opportunity to buy and develop land. Perhaps in a new place Kristin could . . ."

Kristin had clapped her hands over her ears and had run out of earshot, hurt and unwilling to hear another word. A second chance indeed! Why should she have to be like all those girls who spent their entire lives learning to be good wives? Why couldn't she be liked for who she was and not frowned upon because her embroidery stitches were too long and her cakes didn't rise? Was that Mamma's dream—to marry off her daughter? Well, the last thing Kristin would accept was an arranged marriage to someone she didn't like. When and if she ever wanted to marry, she was determined to make that decision to please herself.

The water was beginning to feel colder, and Kristin wanted to get out. She wished Jenny would go back to the house.

Jenny suddenly gasped and said, "Oh, Kristin, your mother sent me here to get you and bring you right back. What if our mothers come looking for us? You'll get into trouble!"

At the thought of what her mother and Fru Berglund would say, Kristin struggled to her feet.

Jenny whirled around and covered her eyes, not moving until after Kristin assured her, "It's all right. I'm dressed."

Jenny turned and said nervously, "They'll guess what happened. Your hair is dripping, but your clothes are dry."

"Oh," Kristin murmured. "I didn't think about that."

Both girls stiffened as they heard voices on the trail.

"They should be down at the lake, Fru Berglund," Mamma was saying. "Linnart said to take this trail and we'd soon find them."

Without a word to Jenny, Kristin picked up her skirts and leaped into the lake.

CHAPTER TWO

❖ ❖ ❖

K RISTIN struggled to her feet just as her mother and Fru Berglund came into view.

Mamma ran forward, crying, "Kristin! What happened to you?"

Kristin shrugged. "One minute I was standing here. The next minute I was in the water." She pushed her dripping hair away from her face and bent to wring out her heavy, waterlogged skirt. She avoided meeting Jenny's eyes. She *knew* she'd laugh.

Fru Berglund immediately took charge. She removed her shawl and wrapped it around Kristin's head and shoulders. "You must get back to the house and into dry clothes," she said. "Jenny and I brought your family a crock of hot potato soup, and that should help."

Kristin, her clothes slapping heavily around her legs, stumbled along the path, the others following in her wake.

Pappa thought the incident was funny. When Mamma explained what had happened, he chuckled and teased

11

Kristin, "How could a nearly grown young lady be so clumsy?"

"It wasn't easy," Kristin answered with a grin. She didn't have the courage to admit to her parents what she had done. *Maybe next time,* she thought. In spite of just having had such a narrow escape, she fully intended to cool off in the lake again.

"Did you bring a change of clothing with you?" Fru Berglund asked Kristin.

Mamma answered for her. "No. She has nothing to change into. We had better return to the Lundgrens'."

"If we did that, we would lose half a day's work, and time is expensive," Pappa protested. "I have a better idea. Upstairs, in the largest bedroom, is a wooden chest filled with clothing. Kristin could go through it and see if there is something in the chest she could wear."

Mamma gasped, but Kristin said, "Mamma, if the clothing is clean, then there is no reason to be afraid of wearing it."

"The people who lived here . . ." Mamma began. "If there are *spöken* unable to leave this house, they may not like your wearing their clothes."

"That is possible." Fru Berglund's expression was as serious as Mamma's.

"We must return to work, *spöken* or no *spöken,*" Pappa announced. "The longer we waste time discussing this matter, the less we will accomplish. Kristin, go upstairs and see what you can find to wear."

Kristin dripped her way through the parlor and up the narrow stairway, breathing quickly as she glanced into the dim, empty rooms. But nothing shifted, nothing sighed. The floorboards creaked only under her own footsteps. Pappa had to be right. Surely there were no *spöken* in the United States.

Kristin easily found the chest and opened it. The clothes smelled slightly musty, but they were clean and neatly folded. Kristin pulled out a woman's skirt, but it ended inches above her ankles, and she would never be able to fasten the waistband. The shirtwaist next to it was tucked with the tiniest of stitches, made for a small-boned woman who probably would have reached no higher than Kristin's ear.

So much for dry clothes. Pappa was going to be *very* unhappy.

As she was about to close the lid of the chest, Kristin glimpsed a piece of rough, dark fabric—too heavy for a woman's dress. She tugged, and out came a pair of men's trousers. With the trousers was a rough, collarless work shirt, exactly like those her father wore. She held the pants up to her waist. The man who lived here had been small, too. These would fit her as would the shirt.

A girl dressed in men's clothing? It was unheard of. Mamma would be shocked! Mrs. Berglund would probably turn purple and collapse in a heap! Kristin grinned. She pulled off her shoes, dropped her wet clothing on the floor in the dust, and climbed into the shirt and trousers. A man's cap lay in the chest, and Kristin clapped it on her head, winding her wet hair and tucking it inside the cap. She glanced into the mirror that hung over a tall dresser and met the eyes of the tall person who looked back at her through a streaked film of dust. Kristin took a few steps and found that she liked the freedom of the trousers and the loose shirt much better than the high-necked, snug-waisted dresses she was used to.

She ran barefoot down the stairs and out to the yard,

coming up behind her mother, who was watching Mrs. Berglund's horses pull their buggy at a steady clip down the dirt road.

"Jenny said to tell you good-bye, and she hoped she'd see you soon," Mamma murmured, her eyes still on the buggy. "One of these days, I hope, our farm will be successful enough so that we can have a pair of horses and a buggy as fine as Fru Berglund's."

Jenny leaned out of the buggy for a last good-bye, and Kristin waved. Kristin saw Jenny stare, then clap her hands over her mouth and almost lose her balance before she dove back inside the buggy.

As Mamma turned and took a good look at Kristin, she shrieked. "Kristin! What do you think you are doing?"

Kristin shrugged. "Pappa told me to put on dry clothes."

"But they're men's clothes!" Mamma put a hand to her forehead and closed her eyes. "Jenny saw you! What will her mother think?"

"She won't know," Kristin said. "Jenny doesn't tell her mother everything."

"Oh? Just how can you be so sure?"

Pappa arrived at a trot from around the corner of the house. "Gerda, what happened?" He came to an abrupt stop as he recognized Kristin.

"Pappa," Kristin said, "the woman's clothes were too small, but the man's fit me perfectly."

Mamma clutched Kristin's arm. "You cannot wear men's clothing! The trousers ... well, they show your limbs."

"It's no secret that I have legs." Kristin tried not to notice that Mamma's face turned pink at Kristin's use of such an unladylike word. "How else could I walk?"

14

"Kristin! What will people think?"

"What people? We're the only ones here," Kristin said.

"Your mother is correct—" Pappa began, but Kristin interrupted.

"If I wear my wet clothes, I might get a cold, but if you let me wear what I have on, I can get a great deal of work done. By the time we are ready to leave, my own clothes will dry again."

The worry wrinkles on Mamma's forehead multiplied, but Kristin hadn't finished. "I'll be working inside the house, anyway. Even if Mrs. Berglund comes back, she won't see me. No one will."

Mamma had opened her mouth to speak, but Pappa answered first. "That's true. No one will see you, and the house must be cleaned. We have wasted enough time. We will all return to work."

Although Mamma's lips were held tightly together in a thin line, she obeyed without further argument. Kristin rinsed the muddy streaks from her clothing and spread the garments in a sunny spot on the grass. Then, while Mamma attacked the wooden back and legs of the sofa with a soft, oily rag, Kristin worked with Pappa on taking the pegs from the beds and unlacing the ropes that crisscrossed the side boards as a support for the mattresses.

As soon as the rooms had been stripped of furniture, Pappa took the mattresses and bedding far from the house and burned them, and Kristin carted a bucket of soapy water and a brush up the stairs.

It wasn't long before she needed to refill the bucket. As she stood at the pump behind the kitchen, vigorously working the handle to slosh water into the bucket, a boy near her own age stepped up beside her. He was broad-shouldered and muscular—no stranger to heavy farm work—and a good four inches taller than Kristin. His hair was a sandy blond, and his skin was tanned from the sun. She gazed back at him with interest.

"I guess that Herr Swensen has already hired someone," the boy said. "I thought I had the job." He studied Kristin's face with a puzzled expression. "You're not from Great Rock Lake. Do you come from over Scandia way?"

"I'm not from Scandia," Kristin answered. "You can say I'm from right here. This very piece of land."

"You're a Swensen, then? I heard they had a daughter, but not a son."

Kristin grinned and pulled off her cap, brushing her tangled hair to one side. "I'm Kristin Swensen," she said as she held out a hand. "I'm Herr Swensen's daughter."

"I'm Johan Olsen." The boy shook Kristin's hand politely, but she could see the surprise in his eyes. "I thought—uh—because of . . . I mean, even so I should have realized . . ."

As his face grew red, Kristin smiled. "I fell into the lake," she told him. "I had to change clothes, and these were the only clothes I could find that would fit."

Kristin could see that Johan was struggling to behave as though seeing a young woman dressed in men's clothing was an everyday occurrence. She could feel her own face grow warm, so she quickly bent to pick up the bucket.

"You'll probably find either Pappa or Mamma around the other side of the house," Kristin said. She looked into Johan's deep-blue eyes. "I hope you won't tell them we've already met. I promised Mamma no one would see me dressed like this."

16

Johan grinned, and his eyes sparkled. "I won't tell them," he answered. "I won't tell anyone. It's *our* secret."

Kristin hurried up the stoop and into the kitchen as quickly as she could with the heavy bucket. She liked Johan's grin. She liked that Johan hadn't said anything terrible about a girl in men's clothing.

Kristin scrubbed the ceilings, walls, and floors even harder, her eyes stinging and her nose burning from the sour, acrid smell of the lye soap, and soon the two bedrooms were spotless. She tackled the storage room next.

Kristin was on her knees, scrubbing the last few feet of space inside the door, when Mamma spoke to her from the stairway. "Here are your clothes, completely dry."

Kristin stood, her shoulders, arms, and legs aching, but made no move to take the clothes from her mother. "See what a good job I've done," she pointed out. "I'll do the hallway next, then the stairs, and soon the entire upstairs will be clean enough to suit anyone, Mamma." She giggled as she said, "Even you."

Mamma smiled and put an arm around Kristin's shoulders. "I'm proud of you," she said, but she twisted to look into the far corners of the room.

"If you're looking for *spöken*," Kristin teased, "you won't find any. The horrible smell of the lye soap has driven them all away."

"Hush, hush! How you talk," Mamma protested, but she sent a searching glance into the nearest bedroom.

Kristin took her mother's free hand and led her into the large bedroom. "This is a nice room," she said. "It overlooks the meadow and stream. We could paint it the light, soft blue you love and put grandmother's quilt on the bed."

Mamma paused as though she were visualizing the room as Kristin had described it, but she sighed and shook her head. "We cannot afford paint right now. Painting the house, both inside and out, will come much later. We have livestock to buy and crops to plant." Her voice suddenly broke.

Kristin was startled to see tears in her mother's eyes.

"I'm sorry," Mamma said. "We are very far from home, and I miss my mother."

"I miss *Mormor,* too," Kristin said.

Impulsively she wrapped her arms around Mamma and held her tightly. "I'm going to write to *Mormor* tonight," she said. "There's so much to tell her."

For just an instant Mamma sagged against Kristin's shoulder, but she soon straightened, businesslike again, and said, "Don't tell her about the mother and children who died in this house." Her glance shifted again toward the corners of the room.

"I know," Kristin said. "*Mormor* would worry about *spöken,* too."

"And why shouldn't she?" Mamma demanded. "Didn't she see with her own eyes her best friend, Ruta, who appeared to her moments after death? And your great-uncle, Carl, when he worked in the palace, saw the *vita frun* coming toward him one dark night."

"*Vita frun*! As Pappa said, there may be ladies in white roaming the halls of the Swedish palace," Kristin said, "but not in the United States. There are no castles or palaces here."

"*Spöken* can be anywhere."

For an instant Kristin felt cold chills along her backbone. "Don't talk about *spöken,* Mamma. Please!"

Mamma sighed. "I can only hope that the spirit of the

mother who died in this house has left in peace along
with the spirits of her babies. But if she still has ties
here that are not broken, if she is searching for her husband—"

"Mamma, don't!" The sun was low in the sky, and
Kristin found herself peering nervously into the shadows.

"Let us hope the spirits will not bring us bad luck,"
Mamma said.

"Pappa says our luck is what we make it." Kristin tried
to sound convincing, at least to herself.

The front door slammed, and they both jumped.

"Gerda! Kristin!" Pappa called. "It is time to return to
town. Are you ready?"

Mamma thrust Kristin's clothing into her arms. "It's
wrinkled, but it will serve," she said. "Hurry and change.
If your father's young worker is still here, it would never
do to let him see you this way."

Kristin took her clothes into the smaller bedroom and
struggled into them. Compared with the shirt and trousers, the high neck of the dress was snug, its long sleeves
binding. The yards of material in the skirt hung heavily
around Kristin's legs. Before she trotted down the stairs
to join her parents, she draped the man's clothing over a
peg that had been hammered into one wall. She was
going to enjoy wearing the clothes again—it had made
her work so much easier.

The parlor had been transformed. Its furniture had
been put back into place, the wood gleaming as though
it had known nothing but years of loving care. Once
Mamma hung curtains at the windows and colorful hang-
ings on the walls, the room would begin to look cheerful.

In the front yard Kristin walked past the scattered
pieces of furniture from the upstairs and met her father

at the wagon. Johan had hitched the horses in place and stood next to them, holding the reins.

Pappa introduced Johan to Kristin. As they formally shook hands, Kristin tried to ignore the admiration in Johan's eyes.

She climbed demurely up on the wagon seat and sat waiting for her parents. The cradle, its wood now gleaming, rested in the back of the wagon. It was filled with the contents of the chest. Obviously Mamma wanted those reminders of the previous tenants out of her house. To Kristin's dismay, however, Mamma hurried through the front door with the clothing Kristin had borrowed and tossed it into the back of the wagon. Mamma sat on Kristin's right with her no-nonsense look, and Kristin knew she had lost any chance of wearing those clothes again.

"We will see you tomorrow, bright and early," Pappa said to Johan.

"When you're ready to plow, I'll bring my father's team," Johan answered. "The plowing should go easily, even though the land has lain fallow for over two years."

Pappa gave Johan a wave as he guided the horses across the drive and into the road.

"Now let's practice our English," Kristin suggested.

"We are all very tired," Mamma answered.

"But we'll forget the language if we don't use it." She tried to enlist her father's support. "Pappa, you are the one who insisted that we learn English."

"I know," he said, "and I still believe it is a good idea to know the language. I just wasn't aware that we would be living in such a large Swedish settlement."

"But if we speak English when we are together—"

Mamma interrupted, and Kristin could hear the exhaustion in her voice. "Please, Kristin, be patient. Later . . . perhaps in the evenings."

"I am pleased with the young man I hired," Pappa said. "Johan Olsen is a fine boy from a good family, I've been told. His father is strict, but his rules are fair. Johan will never get into trouble if he pays attention to his father. You can be sure of that."

Kristin twisted to face her father. "Pappa! Do you mean that Johan can only be considered a good boy if he does exactly what his father wants him to do?"

Pappa let out a long, exaggerated sigh. "Kristin, I am too tired to argue," he said.

Kristin forgot about arguing as she took a good look at her father. "You're wet!" she cried. "Your hair is dripping, and your shirt is sticking to your shoulders."

"While you and your mother were finishing your chores, I took the opportunity to rinse off in the lake."

"What a good idea. Tomorrow Mamma and I should do it."

Mamma gasped. "Kristin! It's bad enough even to think of such a thing! It's even worse to say it aloud!"

"But if Pappa can rinse off in the lake, then why can't we?" Kristin knew her words would be provoking to her mother—but she also knew her mother couldn't resist an argument any more than Kristin could.

"You should know by now that women cannot do everything that men do," Mamma said. "It has always been so."

"Who made that rule? Once you think of it, you wonder why."

Pappa groaned, and Mamma said, "We will have no more discussion of these foolish questions and ideas. Forget about these things and be our loving, good daughter."

Kristin remembered the coolness of the water against her skin, the freedom of splashing in her own private pool. *Why can't women do the same things as men?* she thought with disappointment. Wasn't life supposed to be different in the United States?

CHAPTER THREE

❖ ❖ ❖

THAT night, before she went to sleep on a pallet in a corner of the Lundgrens' parlor, Kristin began a letter to her grandmother:

> *Beloved Mormor, we have a house! And furniture! Everything was filthy and covered with more dirt and dust than you can imagine, but we have been scrubbing and polishing, and soon all will be beautiful—not as fine as our house at home . . .*

Kristin scratched out the words *at home,* substituting, *in Sweden.* A rush of homesickness for her grandmother brought tears to her eyes. As she rubbed them away, she glanced at the nearby table on which she'd placed the six-inch hand-carved wooden Dalarna horse *Mormor* had given her as a parting gift. The horse—resplendent in its shiny red lacquer and ornately painted mane, bridle, and saddle—had been given to her grandmother when she was a girl, so it was a special, well-loved treasure she had passed on to Kristin.

In two days it would be Kristin's seventeenth birthday. *Mormor* would have baked an apple cake or made a steamed pudding filled with raisins, and the entire family would have gathered around to laugh and eat and wish Kristin another year of happiness. No one could imagine how terribly much she missed her grandmother!

As soon as we move into our house, I'll put the little Dala-horse in a place of honor—somewhere I can see him each day, because he'll remind me of you.

Kristin went on to tell her grandmother she'd met a friend, Jenny, but sleep was so demanding that she promised herself she'd finish the letter the next evening. It would be ready for the mail packet Herr Lundgren took each week to the post office in Scandia. She crawled between the down-stuffed comforters that made up her pallet and slept soundly.

During the next two days Kristin and her parents worked from sunup to sundown on the house, stopping only to eat the midday food and take a short rest. Johan joined them, but there was little time for talk.

Finally the house was ready to live in. Pappa purchased a wagon and a large, strong horse to pull it, and Mamma packed their belongings. As Mamma and Fru Lundgren hugged each other tightly, the Swensens repeated the traditional words of gratitude over and over again: *"Tack för i dag! Tack för i dag!"*

Kristin and her parents arrived at their new home to find the windows shining in the late-afternoon sunlight, reflecting the greens and blues of the meadow and stream.

Wide floor planks gleamed around the edges of two colorful rag *trasmattor* and one *ryamattor* with its woolly nap—a generous gift from Fru Lundgren and the ladies of Great Rock Lake's Lutheran church. Cupboard drawers were packed with the Swensens' linens and clothing, suits and dresses were ironed and hung in the wardrobes, food filled the shelves in the small pantry, and a vase of soft yellow dog's-tooth violets adorned the parlor table. Kristin stood her Dala-horse in a place of honor on a low kitchen shelf.

To Kristin's surprise Mamma unwrapped a plump apple cake, fragrant with nutmeg and cinnamon, and placed it in the center of the table. "We would not forget your birthday," Mamma said with a smile. "Fru Lundgren baked this for you because I told her how much you'd miss your grandmother's cake."

For just an instant Kristin was surrounded by the warm, spicy smells of her grandmother's kitchen. She saw *Mormor* lift the golden cake from the oven, top it with a special brown sugar, butter, and cream mixture, and return it to the oven to brown. Kristin heard her own laughter as—after everyone had eaten—she'd snatch up the extra piece *Mormor* always made sure was there and race from the house down the grassy slope to the lake, and she felt the soft sweetness of her grandmother's arms around her in a special birthday hug.

Birthdays would never be the same.

Pappa beamed and reached for a knife to cut the cake. "Moving into our new home on Kristin's birthday should be a good omen," he said. He handed the first slice to Kristin. "Many happy wishes, daughter."

"Thank you," Kristin said, and tried to smile.

Mamma took a bite of her slice and exclaimed, "What a delicious cake!"

But it was not *Mormor*'s cake, and to Kristin it was heavy and lumpy and hard to swallow. She had expected America to be very different from Sweden, but here in Minnesota it was almost exactly like living in Sweden— only without her loving *Mormor*.

Mamma savored the last crumb of her cake and said, "Tomorrow we'll see the Lundgrens at church."

Kristin knew that her mother was looking forward to going to church for more than one reason. Mamma had met just a few of the women in Great Rock Lake; after church services she would be able to meet the rest of the women who lived in the area.

"Women need each other," Mamma had once told Kristin. "Even though a woman's life revolves around her husband, only another woman can truly understand how she thinks and feels."

Kristin looked forward to seeing Jenny Berglund again . . . and to seeing Johan. He would be at church with his family, and perhaps during the afternoon they'd have a better chance to become acquainted than they'd had under the eyes of her parents. The mischief in Johan's eyes intrigued Kristin.

By Sunday morning the heat had broken, and the air was cool and clear. The Swensens rose before the sun came up so that the animals could be well cared for and the necessary chores done before they left for church services.

"Pastor Jon Holcomb is somewhat different from the Lutheran pastors we knew in Sweden. He takes time to greet everyone after services and chat a bit," Fru Lundgren had told them. "I remember that our pastor in Sweden always disappeared immediately after services. Anyone who wanted to talk to him had to make an appointment."

Mamma had nodded. "Our dean was the same, a very formal but well-respected man." She'd suddenly looked puzzled. "If this is how things are done in America, we will have to get used to it, but it will seem strange to chat with a pastor. What should we chat about?"

Fru Lundgren had smiled as she'd replied, "Never fear, Pastor Holcomb will pick a topic."

The Swensens passed the grade school and the teacher's quarters on their way to the Lutheran church, which stood high on a hill in the center of the town of Great Rock Lake. Beyond the church's cemetery was an unpaved main street with wide wooden sidewalks on both sides. To the north was a blacksmith's shop, a harness shop, a lumber company, and large lumber shed. Farther on were a mill, a grain elevator, and a large warehouse. To the south was the Lundgrens' general store flanked by a milliner's shop and the town bank. The names of the establishments, hand-painted in English, were only slightly more prominent than their proprietors' Swedish names.

Nodding and smiling at occupants of the other wagons and buggies, even though many faces were unfamiliar, the Swensens made their way to the Lutheran church.

The frame church, painted white inside, with a colorful trim around the walls and behind the altar, was almost filled. Men and boys in dark suits sat on one side of the aisle, while on the other side sat the women and girls dressed in black or brown with hats or bonnets in the same dark shades. Only the small children, in their white dresses or rompers, brightened the somberly dressed congregation. As the Swensens arrived and an usher led them down the aisle to seats close to the front, Kristin felt all eyes upon them.

Mamma nodded politely to the woman seated on her left, and the woman nodded in return. Kristin, who had immediately spotted Jenny with her family, felt more at ease. She took one of her mother's hands, which was damp with nervous perspiration, and stroked it gently. *It's all right, Mamma,* she wished she could say. *You're a wonderful, kind, generous person, and these women will love you. You'll soon have many new friends.*

With a pang Kristin remembered the two good friends she had made on the ship coming to the United States. The voyage in steerage, with its stinking hold and miserable food, would have been unbearable without Rose and Rebekah. Kristin pictured the two of them: Rose, her red hair sparkling in the sunlight, and Rebekah, her smile warm and caring.

They had arrived at Ellis Island late in April. Surely by now Rose would be working to help bring her mother and younger sisters to Chicago, and Rebekah . . . Kristin hoped with all her heart that Rebekah was going to school, getting the education she wanted so much.

The promise Kristin had made that one day they'd all be together again was a promise she would never forget. It would happen. She would *make* it happen.

Kristin jumped as Mamma's elbow jabbed her ribs. She came back to the present with a start and watched a large man with thick gray hair and a ruddy face stride to the altar—black robe flapping around his shoes. The members of the congregation rose to their feet, hymn books in hand.

They vigorously sang the Swedish national anthem, while a plump, dark-haired woman bent over the church organ, her elbows bobbing up and down like chicken wings as she played. A familiar Swedish hymn came next; then the service began. Eventually the pastor climbed the stairs to the pulpit and delivered a thunderous and overly long sermon about Judgment Day—in Swedish of course.

By the time the two-hour service ended, Kristin was so hungry, her stomach rumbled. Hoping that no one could hear it, she smiled and shook hands with countless people whose names she'd never be able to remember, until at last Pappa brought their basket of food from the wagon and they all joined the other families at tables and benches set out on the lawn.

Although from time to time Johan glanced over at Kristin and smiled, he remained with his parents and his four younger brothers and sisters. Johan's parents had been friendly when they'd been introduced. His father was a muscular, jovial man, his hair thinning to wisps on top; his mother, busily keeping her younger children in hand, let her husband do most of the talking.

Just as Kristin thought she couldn't eat another bite, the Berglunds came to the Swensens' table with ginger cake. In return Mamma passed a plate of the flaky butter cookies she'd been famous for at home.

"Come with me," Jenny whispered to Kristin. "There are some friends of mine who want to meet you now, before the Young People's Society has its get-together."

She led Kristin past the carved stones in the church graveyard to a grassy, shaded knoll on which a group of girls—dressed properly in dark, high-necked, long-sleeved dresses—was seated. Kristin guessed that they ranged in age anywhere from fifteen to eighteen.

There was an excited murmur and wiggle as Kristin and Jenny approached. Kristin stopped and grabbed Jenny's arm, nearly pulling her off her feet. "What have you told them about me?" she asked.

"Not much," Jenny said, but her glance was evasive. "I haven't known you long."

"You didn't tell them about my swimming in the lake, did you?"

"Don't you think I can keep a secret?"

Unconvinced, Kristin asked, "Did you tell them I wore men's clothing?"

"I didn't promise to keep *that* secret," Jenny said. Before Kristin could answer, Jenny exclaimed, "Oh, Kristin! You don't know how exciting you are. We've never met anyone like you before."

As Kristin and Jenny approached, the girls jumped up and clustered around them, introducing themselves.

"So tell!" a plump girl named Freda blurted out. She glanced at Jenny. "Jenny wouldn't tell us what, but she said you do all sorts of interesting things, like wearing men's clothes. What other exciting things do you do?"

"I've been working hard helping to get our house ready to live in," Kristin said, evading the question. "I wouldn't call that exciting."

Ida, one of the pair of twins, looked disappointed. "We all help clean house. We want to know about the other things you do."

Kristin decided she might as well discover right this minute if these girls would want to be her friends. "I like to fish," she said, "and I like to ride bareback, and I hate to embroider, and I'm a terrible cook."

Clara who was obviously the youngest of the girls, shrugged. "What's so exciting about that?" she asked. "I don't like to embroider, either, and sometimes I go fishing with my brothers."

A couple of the other girls nodded agreement.

Kristin looked at them curiously, and asked, "Is it because you live in the United States? In my town in Sweden it's so different. All the girls are supposed to do is learn how to be good wives and talk about getting married."

Josie, who looked to be the eldest, answered, "What's so terrible about learning how to cook and sew and wanting to get married?"

"We all want to get married," a tall girl called Esther said. "Either a girl marries and has a husband to take care of her, or she's an old maid."

"That's right," Freda said.

From the expressions on the girls' faces Kristin knew she was outnumbered, but she said, "Getting married is fine if you're in love. In Sweden many marriages are arranged and a girl has to live with her parents' choice."

"Many marriages are here, too," Jenny said, "but it's not quite as common as my mother says it is in Sweden, thank goodness. I don't think I'd like an arranged marriage."

Clara grinned as she teased, "That's because you're always falling in love. It's Paul, this time, isn't it?"

"Never mind," Jenny answered, and the others laughed.

"I like what I'm finding out about this country," Kristin said. "I think women really must have more freedom here. I heard that in four western states—Wyoming, Colorado, Idaho, and Utah—women can vote. Do you know if that's true?"

Esther made a face. "Of course we know that, but who cares? I don't know why women would want to vote.

Men take care of things like that, and as far as I'm concerned, they're welcome to them."

The twins nodded agreement, but Josie said to Kristin, "You sound like Fru Dalquist's sister who visits here from Minneapolis. In fact, she's here today. I saw her. She even gives speeches about how women in *all* the states should have the right to vote. My father says she's crazy."

"Who's Fru Dalquist?" Kristin asked.

Ida broke in. "Fru Dalquist is our church organist. Her sister is named Sigrid Larson—*Fröken* Larson. She's ages and ages old, and she never married."

All the girls stared at Kristin. "Fröken Larson probably never wanted to marry," she said.

"Every woman wants to marry," Minnie—Ida's twin—insisted.

"My mother's aunt, Lucia, never married," Freda said. "She went from her brothers' houses to ours and back again, helping with the mending and the sewing and watching the children. Someone always had to take care of her because she didn't have a husband to do it."

"No one has to take care of Fröken Larson," Jenny pointed out. "She teaches at the University of Minnesota."

Kristin scrambled to her feet.

"Where are you going?" Jenny asked.

"Josie said she's here," Kristin explained. "I'm going to meet Fröken Larson."

CHAPTER FOUR

❖ ❖ ❖

THE other girls followed Kristin back to the area where the adults were still chatting and eating, but they drifted away as Jenny took Kristin by the hand and led her to the table where Fröken Larson, a tall, thin woman whose blond hair was beginning to be streaked with white, sat beside her sister.

After the introductions came pleasantries. Kristin remarked on how well Fru Dalquist played the organ, and Fru Dalquist claimed she spoke for many when she said how pleased they all were that the Swensen family had chosen to move into their midst. Fröken Larson praised Fru Swensen's butter cookies, and Jenny said she hoped Fröken Larson's visit to Great Rock Lake would be a long and pleasant one.

"Please sit with us and visit," Fröken Larson said.

As she scrambled over the bench and tugged her skirt into place, Kristin said in a quiet voice, "I was told that you believe that women should be able to vote."

"Yes, I do," Fröken Larson answered. "I'm one woman out of many who are working for national suffrage."

Fru Dalquist rolled her eyes as she quickly jumped to her feet. "Please excuse me," she said. "There is someone I must talk to."

Jenny patted Kristin's shoulder. "I'll see you later," she said. "Paul Erickson just arrived with some others from Scandia." As an afterthought she asked, "Would you like to meet Paul?"

"Later, thanks," Kristin told her.

Jenny grinned, and hurried in Paul's direction.

Kristin leaned toward Fröken Larson. "Women are really *working* to get the vote nationally? How do they do this?"

Fröken Larson settled herself on the bench and asked, "Have you ever heard of Susan B. Anthony?"

"No," Kristin answered.

"Miss Anthony believes so strongly that women should have the right to vote that she defied the law and was arrested and tried in court for her beliefs."

Kristin gasped. It was hard to take this in; Mamma would never understand any of it. "What happened to her, Fröken Larson?"

Fröken Larson looked at Kristin with kindness as she said, "I believe we will be friends, Kristin, and friends should not be so formal, no matter how strong the traditions of our native country. Please call me Sigrid."

"All right . . . Sigrid." At least Kristin had met someone who was not afraid to break tradition. She wondered if Sigrid Larson had ever cooled off in a lake or worn men's clothing. "Do you speak English?" Kristin asked.

"Of course," Sigrid said. "I'm glad to discover that you do, too. That gives us one more thing in common."

"Then could we speak in English, please?" Kristin asked. "I need the practice, and everyone here seems to want to speak Swedish."

Still speaking Swedish, Sigrid answered, "While we are at this gathering, with many others around us, we should speak in the language they understand. We wouldn't want them to think us rude in setting ourselves apart."

Kristin wished she had thought of that before she had spoken. "I'm sorry," she said. "But I just don't understand why the people who emigrated here don't try to be like the rest of the people in the United States."

"Like which people? The Germans, who have a large settlement of their own in Minneapolis? The Norwegians? The Italians? The French?"

Kristin was surprised. "Do you mean they speak their own languages? They don't speak English?"

"Many of them learn English. They have to if they're going to do business with the others, but they speak their native tongues in their homes. The children of the immigrants, however—many of whom were born here—are quicker than their parents in picking up the language."

"But how can the children learn to speak English well if no one else speaks it?"

"By law, children learn English in school, but this is a Swedish community, Kristin. The people who live here came to this area to be among their own people, and they speak Swedish because they are comfortable with it. It's also an important tie to the land from which they came. They don't want to lose it, and they don't want their children to lose it. You'll find that a 'Swede school' is held each summer for school-age children so that they'll be proficient in the language."

Kristin still didn't understand why people who chose

to come to a new country tried to make it exactly like the country they had left, but she was more impatient to learn all she could about women's suffrage. "Will you tell me more about Susan B. Anthony?" she asked.

Sigrid nodded. "When Miss Anthony attempted to vote, the all-male jury followed the judge's order to find her guilty as charged. But she did not serve time in jail.

"Before Miss Anthony was sentenced, she told the judge that the courts were wrong. She said they had been wrong on other occasions as well. They had been wrong when they said it was a crime to give a cup of cold water or a crust of bread to an escaping slave making his way to Canada. And they were just as wrong when they robbed women of the fundamental privilege of citizenship—the right to vote."

"I would think that with that logic the judge had to agree with her," Kristin said.

"He didn't. He ordered Miss Anthony to pay a fine. She refused and challenged him to either hold her in custody or send her to jail until it was paid. He refused to do either, because putting her in jail would have enabled her to take her case to the highest court in the nation— the United States Supreme Court. If the Supreme Court judges disagreed with the state jury, they could have forced the state to let all women—not just Miss Anthony—vote in all elections."

"How long has Miss Anthony been working for women's rights?" Kristin asked.

"Since 1853."

Kristin gulped. "But it's 1902!"

"Much has been accomplished, but a change as drastic as women's suffrage takes time."

"I have so much to learn about this country and all that is possible here," Kristin said with a sigh.

"You can begin now. I have a book at home that would be good for you to read. I'll be coming back to Great Rock Lake at least once before Midsommarfest. I'm pleased to lend it to you. I'll also be glad to tell you more about Miss Anthony's work. She helped found the National American Suffrage Association, to which I belong. We have a chapter in Minneapolis."

"Does Miss Anthony come to any of the meetings?"

"No. Miss Anthony is eighty-two years old now and doesn't travel as much as she once did. However, if she, or one of her associates, such as Anna Shaw, does travel here to speak, perhaps you would like to come to Minneapolis to hear her. I'd be very happy to have you stay with me."

Go to Minneapolis? The city was one of the pair of beautiful cities that had entranced Kristin while she and her family had waited to change trains. Kristin had loved everything she saw as her family rode in a buggy through Minneapolis and its twin city across the Mississippi River, Saint Paul. Kristin bounced to her feet. "I would love to come! Thank you! Thank you!"

"With your parents' permission of course."

Kristin knew the look on her face must have given away her thoughts because Sigrid smiled and said, "When the time comes, I'll speak to your parents and be as persuasive as I can in inviting you for a visit."

"Maybe if your sister . . . if Fru Dalquist also tries to persuade them . . ."

"Unfortunately my sister doesn't share my political views. You'd be surprised how many women are afraid of change. They'd rather be taken care of—no matter how poorly—than enjoy equality."

"What about the women in the western states that let them vote? They must not have been afraid."

Sigrid smiled. "After what they went through to help settle and civilize the western territories, I'm sure they weren't afraid of anything," she said.

"Most of the women here in Great Rock Lake already made a big change when they came here from Sweden," Kristin said. "And yet my own mother doesn't want to change! She doesn't understand. She was horrified when I wore men's clothes."

Sigrid's expression didn't alter as she asked, "Why did you?"

"My own clothes were wet, and there was nothing else to fit me." Kristin stopped, too embarrassed to tell the whole story. "Mamma was afraid I'd shock people."

"Your mother is right. If you attempt something too daring, you will. When Amelia Bloomer invented a costume with trousers for women and she and Miss Anthony wore them, people were so upset, they threw eggs at them."

In surprise Kristin asked, "Do you mean that I wasn't the first woman to wear trousers?"

Sigrid said quietly, "Change takes time, Kristin, and it must be done properly, not impulsively. When people know, like, and trust you, they're more ready to listen to your ideas."

She glanced behind Kristin and murmured, "Pastor Holcomb keeps looking over this way. I think that he wants to talk to you, but he's uncomfortable conversing with me. Why don't you join your parents, and I'll see you later."

"Today?"

"Next time I'm in town, I'll stop by your house with the book I told you about. I'd like to meet your parents, too."

Kristin reluctantly left the table and walked to where her parents were standing with Pastor Holcomb. Without his flapping black robes he was far less intimidating, and Kristin shook his hand without flinching.

His eyes probed Kristin's as though he could read her thoughts as he questioned her about her childhood and her participation in the Lutheran church. Finally he expressed his pleasure that she had been confirmed and had full membership in the church.

"Your father has told me that he thinks it would benefit you to become involved in the activities of our church," he said. "As it happens, our teacher for Sunday's primary class has not been well, and I planned to ask one of the girls to substitute for the next few weeks. However, your father assured me you could handle the children and are well versed. Will you take our four- and five-year-olds and teach them their religion—beginning next Sunday?"

Kristin wished her father had asked her permission before volunteering her but she answered politely, "I've never taught. I wouldn't know how or what to teach them."

"We have instructions for you to follow," Pastor Holcomb said. "I will give you the material before you leave this afternoon. It will be a good way for you to join our community."

Teaching small children their religion was not exactly how Kristin had planned to spend her Sundays, but pride shone in Pappa's eyes, and Mamma smiled with delight.

Since Kristin had hesitated, Pastor Holcomb urged, "It will not be difficult. Most of the little ones have given up their baby lisps and speak our language well."

"English?" Kristin asked with excitement.

"No, *our* language. Swedish."

Kristin realized she'd have to say yes, but then thought with excitement, *Why should they speak Swedish? I can teach them in English! They'll have the advantage of learning both their religion and English, and this will keep me from forgetting the language!*

"I shall be very happy to teach them," she answered Pastor Holcomb.

CHAPTER FIVE

❖ ❖ ❖

As Pastor Holcomb left to chat with others in his flock, Kristin's parents were captured by the Lundgrens. Kristin wandered away from the group, wondering if she should go in search of Jenny.

"Kristin, wait!" Johan hurried to her side, but once there, seemed tongue-tied. "You—uh—you look very nice today."

"Better than in my dusty working clothes, you mean?"

His face reddened. "That's not what I meant."

Kristin rested her fingertips on his arm and grinned. "I know. I was just teasing."

He grinned back. "Have you seen much of the town? Or of the lake? There's a good view of this end of Great Rock Lake from the hill behind the church."

"I'd like to see it," Kristin said. "But what about the Young People's Society? Won't it be meeting soon?"

"We'll have plenty of time."

As they walked past the tables, Johan's father glanced up from his conversation with Herr Dalquist and studied

41

Kristin. Puzzled, Kristin stared back, and he quickly nodded and smiled before he turned away.

Johan, who was busy telling Kristin about the good lake fishing for bass and carp, hadn't noticed.

"I like to fish," Kristin told him as they rounded the corner of the church and strolled up the hillside.

"You do?" Johan looked surprised. "I know a couple of very young girls who sometimes go fishing with their brothers, but it's not something most girls your age do."

"My father used to take me fishing when I was younger," Kristin said. "For lake fishing we'd sometimes dig for worms and sometimes use minnows."

"You don't mind putting a worm on a hook?"

"Of course not."

Johan smiled. "You're not like other girls, are you?"

"I don't know," Kristin teased. "Maybe you'd better tell me. What are other girls like?"

"I didn't bring you here to talk about other girls." Johan reached for her hand and pulled Kristin up to a flat promontory. "There's a good view of the lake here," he said, dropping her hand.

Kristin moved close to Johan, aware of the steep drop in front of them, and he put an arm around her waist to steady her. The grassy slopes fell away to dark clumps of pine, and beyond the forest a broad expanse of water glimmered silver-blue in the sunlight. As though something had startled them, a swarm of blackbirds swooped loudly from the pines, shooting into the air with beating wings and circling over the lake before choosing another place to settle.

"It's beautiful," Kristin murmured.

"Yes," Johan agreed. "There's something special about

this place. I've been told it's very much like the southern area my parents came from in Sweden."

Kristin sighed. "Everyone keeps comparing everything here with the way it was in Sweden and trying to make this part of the United States exactly like Sweden. I didn't think you'd do it, too."

She could hear the surprise in Johan's voice. "I don't even remember Sweden. I was only a baby when my parents brought me to the United States. My brothers and sisters were born here, and I imagine we'll all live here the rest of our lives."

Kristin turned to glance up at him. "Don't you want to see other places?"

"Maybe, in travel," Johan said, "but where could I find better land to farm?"

"You want to be a farmer, doing just what your father does." It wasn't a question, and Kristin felt a jolt of disappointment as she stated the fact, but Johan didn't seem to notice and smiled.

"Yes, I want to farm, but not as my father does. His father was content with a small farm in Sweden, but my father came to America because of his love of the land. He knew he could develop a good-sized farm and keep it productive."

Johan looked down the valley as though he were seeing something else. "My grandfather's farm was small," he said, "because there was only so much a man could accomplish with simple hand tools. My father, however, can make use of machines, like his steam-driven threshing machine. It's more help than four farmhands."

His enthusiasm growing, Johan went on. "Some of the larger cities have electricity, Kristin. Someday it will be brought out to the rural areas. Can you imagine what electricity can do for farmers?"

"Uh—not exactly," Kristin said.

"Think about the milk separator, for example. It has to be cranked for what seems like hours, but it could be operated by electricity."

"Do you know how to do it?"

"No, but someone will figure it out and much more. I've read about automobiles that run on a fuel called gasoline. The people who design and build farm equipment—can't you see them developing machines that run on gasoline to help farmers? Maybe an even better threshing machine."

Kristin couldn't picture it at all, but Johan's enthusiasm was intriguing. "Is that what you want to do, Johan? Do you dream of inventing farm machinery?"

Johan chuckled. "No. I'll leave that up to others. There's a good feeling about owning land and working to make it thrive. A man's land can feed his family, it can produce crops of wheat, corn, and potatoes and provide grazing for cattle, sheep, and horses. It's solid under his feet. It's a piece of the earth that belongs only to him. My dream is what I see coming in the future—wheat fields that stretch for miles and miles in this vast country, farms in the United States large enough to supply the world with food because machines will be invented to supply the labor." He stopped and looked embarrassed. "I didn't mean to go on like that."

"There's nothing wrong with loving the work you do."

"I wouldn't call the way I feel about the land *loving* it." The mischievous twinkle appeared in Johan's eyes, and his arm tightened about Kristin's waist as he said, "*Loving* is the way I'd feel about a beautiful girl."

Kristin tried to sidestep, but there wasn't much room on the promontory. "Any beautiful girl?"

"No. It would be a very special girl."

Kristin glanced at the drop below their feet. "Sometime you must tell me all about this special girl, but not here and now, when we're likely to fall off the top of this mountain."

Johan laughed. He released Kristin, jumped down from their perch, and reached to help her down.

As he took her hand and led her back toward the church, he said, "Tell me about the things you like to do. Do you weave and embroider? I bet you're already a good cook."

So he is just like everyone else! Kristin thought. *He believes the only job for a girl is to become a housewife!* Rebelliously Kristin said, "I like to sing." The memory of Rose on board ship dancing a fast Irish jig to the tune of her uncle's fiddle popped into Kristin's mind. "And I think it would be great fun to learn to dance."

Johan chuckled. "Dance? That's a good joke! Imagine what our pastor would have to say if he caught you twirling around the room! He's pretty rigid about any kind of dance except traditional folk dancing."

Kristin shrugged and smiled at Johan as she said, "My voice may not be the best, but at least Pastor Holcomb could find nothing *morally* wrong with my singing."

"That depends," Johan said. "If you sang in the Lutheran church, he'd beam with approval; but if you added your voice to the Methodists, you'd find out how indignant he can get."

Kristin stopped and stared at Johan. "Why in the world would I sing with the Methodists?"

"They have a church not far from here," he said, "and

last month they began what they call a singing school for young people on Wednesday evenings."

"A singing school? They teach hymns?"

Johan smiled broadly. "I understand they throw in a hymn or two, but they have song sheets with the words of popular songs on them. There's a new one called 'In the Good Old Summertime.' " He hummed a couple of bars.

"Johan! How do you know all this?"

"One of our neighbors is Methodist, and they have a son who's a friend of mine. Want me to sing the words for you?"

Matching his own mischief, Kristin said, "Instead why don't you take me to this singing school?"

Johan stopped and studied Kristin's face. *He doesn't know if I'm serious or not,* she thought, and it was hard to keep from bursting into laughter.

"Go to the Methodists?" he asked. "You're joking, aren't you?"

Kristin managed to keep a straight face. "It's not as though we were joining their church. There's nothing wrong with singing, and even though I've never met one, I'm sure there's nothing wrong with Methodists."

Johan rubbed his chin and frowned a little. "But Pastor Holcomb strongly disapproves."

With a swish of her skirts Kristin turned and began to march back toward the church. "Maybe I'll just go by myself, Johan. I'll tell you all about it and how much fun we had—after I get back."

He hurried to catch up. "Kristin," he said, "let me think about it for a little while. The singing school is going to be held every Wednesday evening during the summer, so we don't have to hurry into a decision."

Kristin couldn't hold back the laughter any longer. She twirled and caught Johan's hands, watching the concern on his face dissolve into a grin.

"You had me fooled," he said. "I guess I still don't understand you."

"Don't try," she answered, and tugged him toward the area where the others were gathered. "Isn't it time for the Young People's Society to be meeting?"

The members of the society—about twenty people from the various Lutheran churches in the area—gathered inside the schoolhouse. After Kristin had been introduced to everyone she hadn't met earlier, there was a short business meeting, presided over by Paul Erickson—the boy from Scandia Jenny had been teased about. He seemed nice, Kristin thought, but in her opinion Johan was much, much nicer. It was voted unanimously that the girls in the society would help make new altar cloths for the small church in Hay Lake, and the boys would repair its leaking roof.

Once the business had been taken care of, three members of the Scandia Club entertained with violin music. After the program, punch and cookies were served, and Kristin heard about the local celebration of Midsommarfest, which would be held on Sunday, June 22, the Sunday closest to the traditional midsummer day of June 24.

"There'll be a bandstand and music," Ida told Kristin.

"And a dinner for the public," Minnie added. "People come from miles around."

"And dress in their native costumes," Clara told her.

"There'll be a maypole," Josie said.

"Just like at home!" Kristin broke in. The maypole dance was her favorite part of Midsommarfest. "With flower garlands hung on the crossbar?"

"What crossbar?" Clara asked.

Jenny explained to Kristin, "Our pole has a circle on top covered in greenery, and the ribbons are fastened below it."

"Don't forget the games and footraces for the children," Esther added, and she asked Kristin, "Did you have these in Sweden?"

"Yes," Kristin said. "And don't you love it when the fiddle music stops and everyone is quiet waiting for the sun to reappear?" She was remembering the magical moment when at midnight the sun barely dipped below the horizon before rising again.

Some of the others looked confused, but Josie explained: "Minnesota isn't as far north as Sweden. You'll find that we have a late twilight, but the sun *does* set."

Paul chuckled at Kristin's wide-eyed bewilderment. "I'm looking forward to the Ost-Kaka pudding with fresh strawberries," he said.

"Do you remember when Arnie Larson got into the strawberries?" Ida asked, and soon everyone was telling stories about previous midsummer festivals, from the time a duck chased a large cricket into Herr Johnson's tuba to the time two-year-old Clara toddled into the lake and five people jumped in to rescue her.

On the drive back to their farm Mamma spoke with excitement about Midsommarfest, impressed with the fact that so many guests came from the twin cities that Fru Sandquist had organized a handicraft booth. For the coming festival Mamma had already agreed to help with the serving of the bountiful dinner and to bring a large pan of Ost-Kaka.

"Kristin," she said, "I volunteered you to help serve,

too. And Linnart—I told them you'd either help set up or take down the tables."

Instead of teasing Mamma with good humor, Pappa surprised Kristin by asking, "How much will this festival cost us?"

Mamma was surprised, too. "Why, whatever it takes to make the Ost-Kaka—a gallon of whole milk, besides the cup of cream and four eggs and—" She broke off. "Why do you ask?"

"The expense of living here is much higher than I had anticipated," Pappa answered. "The parcel of land is large, and the livestock was also fairly costly. I do not want to worry you, but we will not have a crop of wheat or corn this summer to give us much savings."

"What are you saying?" Mamma asked.

"Let me put it this way. Johan has plowed the land for your kitchen garden and a sizable section for our potato crop, and I will no longer have need of his services."

"Oh!" Kristin cried before she thought, and she nearly dropped the books Pastor Holcomb had given her. Mamma shot her a questioning look, so Kristin added meekly, "Johan is hardworking and so helpful we'll miss him."

"You'll see him each Sunday at church," Mamma said calmly, but one eyebrow was still raised.

Pappa went on as though he hadn't heard their conversation. "I am going to require a little extra from both of you," he said. "We will have the cheese and butter you can make from our cows, some of which can be traded for coffee and salt, but we'll need cash in order to purchase the seed for our first wheat crop and for our expenses until the crop is ready to harvest and sell. I have been told that the lumber mills will be hiring full-time in the late fall, after the winter wheat has been planted, and for now I can hire out for short delivery jobs for a Scandia mill that needs its lumber carted to customers in this part of Minnesota."

Mamma sat up stiffly. "You'll be away from home? For long periods of time?"

"Only a few days at a time, no longer than a week," Pappa answered. "This is where the two of you come in. I will not always be on hand to take care of the animals or the potato crop. It means extra work for all of us. I'm sorry it must be this way, but there seems to be no other answer."

"I understand," Mamma murmured.

Kristin said, "Pappa, you know I'm good with animals, and with the land as well."

Pappa nodded, but he kept his eyes straight ahead, and there was a tightness in his voice. "I was sure I would have support from both of you," he told them.

Mamma spoke barely above a whisper, and she gripped her hands together so tightly that her knuckles were white knobs in her pale skin. "When . . . when will all this take place?"

"Not for another few weeks," Pappa said. He glanced down at Mamma and tried to smile. "I'll make sure the repairs on the barn are finished, the potato crop has made a good start, and all is in order before I leave."

For a few moments no one spoke. "Pappa, I'll catch plenty of fish," Kristin finally said. "And with brook trout or lake bass to add to the vegetables from Mamma's garden, we won't have a thing to worry about. We may even have fish to sell."

Pappa frowned down at Kristin. "There will be no selling of fish. I will catch as many fish as possible for you and your mother," he said. "Your mother can salt them to preserve them."

"Why can't *I* catch the fish while you are away?" Kristin demanded. "Or at least go with you and help you catch them?"

"Kristin," Mamma said, "remember that you are a young lady."

"Pappa and I used to go fishing often."

"When you were a child. You are no longer a child. Fishing is not a proper pastime for a young lady."

Kristin squirmed angrily on the hard wagon seat. "Why is it all right for a young lady to fork down hay in the barn and feed the chickens, but it's not all right if she goes fishing?"

Pappa broke into the conversation, his voice firm. "There will be no more discussion about what you will do or not do, Kristin. Your thinking is like that of a child."

"When I was a child, I was allowed to think."

"I said that is enough. Don't make things more difficult for us."

Kristin glanced from her father to her mother and saw that Mamma was close to tears. "I'm sorry," she said. Seeking outside work must have been terribly hard for her father to have to do, and it was obvious that Mamma was already dreading his absences. "I'll try to do everything I can to help," she assured them. "I promise."

"Thank you," Mamma murmured, taking Kristin's hand.

"Your best is what I expect of you," Pappa said.

For a few minutes everyone was silent. Then Mamma

whispered, "This is all the fault of the *spöken* in that house. I knew they would bring us bad luck."

Kristin clung to Mamma's hand the rest of the ride home.

CHAPTER SIX

✦ ✦ ✦

WITHOUT Johan's help Pappa's workload increased, and he often fell asleep in his chair in the parlor soon after he had eaten dinner. He showed Kristin where to graze the cows and how to clean the barn, even though helping with these chores had been an early part of her memories.

"Let me help you now before you go away," she begged, but her father—his face dark with embarrassment—was adamant.

"Until now I've been able to afford to hire extra help when it was needed, so that my wife could devote all her time to woman's work. I regret that you will have to do chores more suited to men while I am away."

"Why should chores be divided into men's work and women's work? Why can't men and women work together until a job is done?"

Pappa sighed. "Why must you challenge *everything*, Kristin?"

"It's not a challenge. It's just an idea that makes sense to me."

"To you perhaps, but to no one else." He rested his hands on her shoulders, and she could see the worry in his eyes. "Please forget these silly ideas of yours and be a good and dutiful daughter to your mother."

"I do try to be a good daughter."

"Being a good daughter is being obedient. Follow your mother's good example."

Kristin sighed as she answered, "All right, Pappa," but she thought, *I can't be a copy of my mother, but I can't be a copy of my father, either. Who can I be?*

How she wished she could talk to Rebekah and Rose to share her thoughts and problems with them—as she had on the ship. Rebekah had been a little apprehensive about her future in New York City, wondering what her life was going to be; and Rose had needed reassurance as she left the train she shared with Kristin's family to Chicago to meet her father and older brothers she hadn't seen in four years. Neither Rebekah nor Rose had known, any more than she, how they'd fit in to this new country or what would be expected of them. But both of them had definite dreams. Rebekah longed to become a teacher and Rose would work to help reunite the family. Kristin stopped and tried to think exactly what her dream was.

Before Kristin went to bed, she wrote to both friends, wishing Rose a very happy birthday. She was already eager to receive her friends' letters back. The United States was such a big country. her friends seemed far away.

In the evenings Kristin studied the lesson books Pastor Holcomb had given her, but she soon put them aside. It was well and good to teach the younger children the basics of their Lutheran religion, but if she was going to teach the lessons in English, then she'd have to familiarize them with the language first.

After services on Sunday, Pastor Holcomb led Kristin into one of the rooms of the parsonage, which had been turned into a Sunday school. She could hear lessons going on in other rooms as she smiled at the dozen youngsters, who smiled back at her. Pastor Holcomb introduced Kristin and admonished the children to behave themselves and learn well before he left her with them.

Kristin immediately said, "We are going to learn about our religion in the English language. How many of you speak English?"

The children stared back at her with wide eyes, and not a single hand was raised.

"Very well," she said, "I am going to say in English, 'My name is Kristin Swensen.' I want you to say the words with your own name. Are you ready?"

A few heads nodded. Kristin repeated the English words, then pointed at a boy seated in front of her. "You say it," she told him.

He stumbled over the first word, but managed to repeat it, adding his name.

"Very good!" Kristin exclaimed. She went to the next child and the next, until all the children had spoken the words correctly.

"Let's play a game," she said. "We'll stand in a circle and say 'My name is' in English, then call out our own names."

The children eagerly jumped to their feet and shouted the words and names at the tops of their lungs.

The door opened, and a stern-faced woman poked her

head into the room. "Are you having a discipline problem?" she asked Kristin.

"Oh, no," Kristin said.

"Do not let the little children get out of hand," the woman said. "The noise is distracting to others."

"I'm sorry," Kristin told her. "It won't happen again."

As soon as the woman disappeared, shutting the door firmly behind her, Kristin said to the children, "Let's go outside. Choose a partner and hold hands and promise me you'll all stay together and won't wander away." As the children giggled and pushed, trying to get in line, Kristin held a finger to her lips. "And be very, very quiet!"

The air was warm and fresh as Kristin led her students out the back garden of the parsonage and across the green, grassy hill. She held out leaves and spoke their names in English. The children recited the words *trees* and *lake* and *grass* until they sprawled in a circle, laughing over *hair* and *nose* and *chin* and *ears*.

"Everything comes from God," Kristin told them, and she recited the first lines of a prayer every Swedish child learned when first able to talk: *"Gud som haver barnen kär, se till mig som liten är."* Translating the words into English, she had them recite after her, "God who loves the children, watch over me, who am little."

It was not long before the children could recite the entire prayer in English. "Good for you!" Kristin cried. She gathered them into a squirming, wiggling hug, laughing as she fell backward onto the grass, some of the children on top of her.

"What is this?"

The deep, stern voice shook Kristin as well as the children, and they scrambled to their feet. Kristin brushed grass from her skirt and said to Pastor Holcomb, "It's such a pretty day, we moved our lesson out-of-doors."

His piercing gaze moved from Kristin to one of the boys near him. "What did you learn in this lesson?" he asked.

The boy, pale with fright, pointed to his face and answered in English, "Chin, ears, nose."

"What!"

Kristin hurried to explain. "I taught them to pray in English. Listen, please, and they'll say a prayer for you."

"No! I do not wish to hear them pray in English, and neither will their parents. Where is the instruction book I gave you?"

"I studied it," Kristin answered, wishing that her heart would stop pounding. "And I'll teach the material, but I want to teach the children in English. That way they can learn both their religion and the language of this country."

"That is not what I requested that you do," he said, his scowl so deep that his eyebrows met in the middle of his forehead.

"But I—"

"You will take the children back indoors and return them to their parents. I will find another teacher for them before next Sunday."

"I'd like to teach them. I'll follow your lesson plan."

Pastor Holcomb shook his head. "I will find another teacher," he repeated.

There was nothing left for Kristin to do but to take the children back to their parents. Then she told her mother and father what had happened—it was better than if they heard it first from Pastor Holcomb.

"It's not fair," Kristin complained. "I did nothing wrong, but he wouldn't give me a second chance."

"The children's parents want them to learn their religion, not how to speak English," Mamma said. "In a way I am glad to know that our pastor is a strict disciplinarian. I've been somewhere afraid that the church in the United States is more lax than it is in Sweden."

Kristin tried not to see the disappointment in her father's eyes. "But I would have taught the children both English and religion," she said.

"You were not asked to teach both," Pappa told her.

Kristin sighed. "Why do the people here cling to the past? They chose to live in this country, didn't they?"

"Many of them had no choice. They came for economic reasons," Pappa said, "just as long ago my great-grandfather emigrated from Norway to Sweden."

"But they're here. So why don't they try to adapt to it?"

Mamma answered, "There is too much that is new. Our comfort is in our own familiar language and our dreams of the past."

"Dreams shouldn't be of the past," Kristin told her. "Dreams are supposed to be about the future."

"Maybe, if you are very young," Mamma said. She took Kristin's hand and enclosed it in both of her own.

Kristin gulped down the hard, burning lump that threatened to close her throat. She and her parents had emigrated to the United States because Pappa had decided they would, and Kristin had decided she would make the best of it. But now it seemed she might not be permitted even to do that.

CHAPTER SEVEN

❖ ❖ ❖

A few days later Pappa left for a hauling job that would take him away from home for three days. "We can use the pay," he said, yet Kristin saw his reluctance to leave as he turned on the wagon seat and gave them a last, longing glance before driving around the bend and out of sight.

"Well," Mamma said as she smoothed down her apron. "There's much to be done, so we had better get to work." Kristin heard the tears behind the words, and she patted her mother's arm.

"I can do Pappa's work as well as my own," Kristin told her. "I used to love to help him with the outdoor chores. He's already milked the cows and sent them out to pasture, so I'll start by cleaning out the barn."

"You'd better wear your father's boots," Mamma said.

Kristin looked down at her long, full skirt. "What good are boots? It's my skirt that's going to sweep through the manure."

Mamma's forehead puckered. "I hadn't thought of

that. We will just launder the dress when you're through with the work."

"I'll have to clean the barn every day," Kristin complained. "No matter how hard we scrub that dress, I'd never want to put it on again." She tried to look nonchalant as she said, "I'll borrow Pappa's clothes."

Momma's eyebrows rose. "That would not be proper."

"Is this the time to worry about what is proper?"

"The people here will not approve."

"It doesn't matter what anyone thinks. Mamma, no one will see me but you. I promise. I'll wear Pappa's clothes only for the dirty work."

Mamma sighed and said, "I have no more strength to argue about it. Wear your father's work clothes if you wish, but remember your promise."

Kristin kissed her mother lightly on the cheek. She collected some pins from Mamma's sewing basket, then ran out to the barn, where she donned her father's big boots, overalls, and work shirt, all of which smelled of sweat mingled with the stink of animals and manure.

She rolled up the pants legs, tucking them into the overlarge boots, and pinned up the sleeves of the shirt. Treading carefully, the boots flopping as she walked, Kristin picked up the long fork and set to work, tossing the heavy mixture of urine-soaked straw and manure onto a pile outside the back door of the barn. In the spring the pile—which would have grown considerably by then—would be forked again, this time into a fertilizer spreader, and be distributed over the planted fields.

Kristin pitched down fresh straw from the loft, surveyed the now-tidy barn, and headed for the privy. She dumped the contents of the chamber pots into the pit and sprinkled in a little lime. She scrubbed the pots, and then, using a stubby straw broom, she scoured the seat and floor of the privy with water thick with melted lye soap. Thankful that the dirtiest and smelliest of the jobs were over, Kristin took off her father's work clothes and hung them in place inside the barn. Gingerly she pulled on her dress and ran back to the house, where a filled pitcher and bowl rested on a bench. She scrubbed her arms, face, and hands with the cold water and a lump of lye soap, then rubbed them dry with the towel that hung on a nearby peg.

Automatically she lugged the pan of soapy water to the kitchen garden and dumped it. The soapsuds would keep away the bugs.

Kristin still had fresh water to pump and carry to the house; split wood to pile next to the huge iron stove in the kitchen; kerosene lanterns throughout the house to collect, clean, and refill; the chickens to feed. In addition, Mamma had used the hand-cranked separator to divide the cream from the milk, and it had to be taken apart and scrubbed free of the cheesy film that coated it.

Mamma opened the back door and called, "I've finished the churning. Would you like a cold glass of buttermilk?"

Exhausted, her arms and shoulders aching, Kristin gulped it down.

"If you'll help me with the stove ashes . . ." Mamma began, but Kristin waved her away. "I can do it," she said as she pulled the heavy drawer from the bottom of the stove. "Do you need them for soap, or should I sprinkle them on the garden?"

"The garden this time," Mamma said. "Some young shoots are up already, and they can use the potash."

Kristin couldn't believe how hungry she was by the

time Mamma called her for the noon meal. She tried to be polite and not wolf down her food, but she ate ravenously.

"You're doing a fine job with the outside chores," Mamma said. "I know it's hard for you to step into your father's shoes."

"I nearly stepped out of them a dozen times," Kristin said with a grin. "I've just begun to realize that the chores I helped Pappa with when I was little were nothing like the job he does every day in running the farm."

"Maybe you should take a rest," Mamma suggested, but Kristin shook her head.

"The kitchen garden needs weeding, and we haven't had rain for a few days, so I'll need to water the potatoes."

"I'll help you," Mamma said, "as soon as I clean the kitchen and start a pot of soup for our supper."

Late in the afternoon Kristin rose from the potato field, stretching and rubbing her back and arms. The cows, bawling because their udders were full, had headed back toward the barn on their own accord. While they drank their fill from the stock tank, Kristin hurried to the barn and scooped a helping of ground meal for each of them into their trough.

As she opened the large barn door, the cow that had assumed the role of leader pushed ahead, the other two following her. They greedily headed for the food, so it was easy for Kristin to fasten them into their stanchions.

Kristin pulled up a clean pail and a stool, seated herself at the side of the first cow, and tied her tail to one hind leg to keep from getting slapped in the face. She wiped the cow's udder with a damp cloth and began to milk her.

She rested her head against the cow's warm side and concentrated on the rhythm of the squeeze and tug and the splash of warm milk into the pail. One of the songs she had heard on the ship coming to America popped into her head, and she milked in time to the meter as she hummed "Yankee Doodle."

Mamma was delighted with the two buckets of milk Kristin carried into the kitchen. "Your father chose the cows wisely," she said. "See how rich the milk is. I'll soon have at least a dozen bricks of butter to trade for Fru Lundgren's groceries."

Mamma's soup was delicious, but Kristin was almost too tired to eat. Two or three times she noticed Mamma glancing nervously toward the parlor, and it puzzled her, but it wasn't until after they had finished eating that Mamma leaned toward her and said softly, "Kristin, the woman who lived and died in this house—I can feel her presence."

Kristin stiffened as chills wriggled up her backbone. The burning wick in the kerosene lamp sent shadows leaping across the walls, and she tried to ignore them. "This isn't her house any longer, Mamma," Kristin said. "It's *our* house. She isn't here."

Mamma went on as though Kristin hadn't said a word. "It's her sorrow. I sense it as if it were my own. Upstairs it hangs like a cloud, and it hovers in the parlor where the cradle once rested."

Kristin involuntarily glanced toward the parlor. "So many people in Sweden believe in *spöken,* you've let them frighten you. Pappa said there are no *spöken* in the United States."

"You and your father may say this," Mamma insisted, "but I know what I feel, and I know the financial difficulties that have come upon us. Who else is to blame but the *spöken?*"

"Why not blame Pappa?" Kristin blurted out. "He's the one who wanted to leave Sweden and come here."

"Kristin!" Mamma looked shocked. "You should respect your father's good judgment."

"I'm sorry, Mamma," Kristin told her, "but I wish you'd stop believing that the spirit of that woman is in this house to do us harm."

"We can't be sure," Mamma murmured.

Kristin reached across the table and took her mother's hands, holding them tightly so that Mamma wouldn't notice the tremors in Kristin's own hands. "Mamma," she said firmly, "you have nothing to be afraid of. I'm here. I'll protect you."

Mamma tried to smile. "I just wish your father were here, too."

"You should have had big strong boys to protect you, instead of one insignificant girl," Kristin teased.

Mamma's eyes clouded over with pain. For an instant she hesitated, then she said, "Kristin, I've never told you. It was too difficult to talk about—too painful even to think about—but you should know. During the years before you were born, I gave birth to three boys—each of them stillborn."

Stunned, Kristin stammered, "Th-three babies? Oh, Mamma, I'm so sorry."

"That's why, when you came along—a fine, healthy baby—we named you Kristin, in honor of the Christ, the Anointed One. You were a special gift to your father and me."

"Oh, Mamma!" Kristin whispered.

Mamma gripped Kristin's hands so tightly, they hurt

as she whispered, "Do you understand what I'm saying? Why you're so important to me? We do not need any more bad luck in this family. If anything should happen to your father or you, I don't know what I would do."

Kristin fought to keep her voice steady. "Nothing bad is going to happen, Mamma," she said, but her mother looked unconvinced.

That night, with the moonlight spilling odd lights and shadows across the room, the usual creakings and poppings of the house seemed strange and foreboding to Kristin. In spite of her exhaustion, and in spite of the fact that she tried to convince herself that she did not—*would not*—believe in ghosts, Kristin found it difficult to close her eyes and fall asleep.

CHAPTER EIGHT

❖ ❖ ❖

IN the morning there was no time to think of *spöken*.
After a breakfast of boiled eggs and bread Kristin
dressed in her cotton work dress, and hurried to the barn
to milk the cows again.

As soon as she had delivered the milk to her mother,
Kristin picked up the stick Pappa used as a prod and led
the cows out to the pasture. The morning air was cool
and fragrant with the sharp tang of the grasses crushed
underfoot. A smattering of yellow buttercups lay scattered across the meadow, pink-and-white lady's slipper
bloomed in the shaded dells, and a pair of startled
meadowlarks sprang from a deep clump of grass and clover, tossing a ripple of notes into the sky.

Kristin paused as the cows began to graze. It was quiet
and peaceful, and she wished she could fling herself down
in the sun-warmed grass and stay forever, but there were
so many, many chores to do.

She strode back to the barn and stopped, startled by
the sound of the manure fork scraping against the hard-

packed floor. "Mamma?" she called, but as she entered the barn, Johan straightened up, wiping an arm across his sweaty forehead, and grinned.

"Oh!" Kristin said. "I thought . . . I mean, why are *you* here, Johan? *What* are you—?"

Johan laughed. "Cleaning a barn is hard work for a girl. I came to help you."

Kristin blushed and stared at the ground. "I don't want you to feel sorry for us," she said. "I can do the work. I don't mind it—"

Johan interrupted. "Kristin, listen to me. I don't feel sorry for you. Many new arrivals have worked for others as your father is doing. This is common here. I came to help because I want to."

"Well . . . as long as you don't feel you *have* to."

There was laughter in his voice as he answered, "Can't you understand? I want to do this for you." He raised the manure fork, studied it as though he'd never seen it before, and said, "However, there has to be a better way of cleaning the stalls and gutters." He paused, thinking. Then his features began to relax again as an idea came to him. "With water," he said thoughtfully. "In great quantities."

"Great quantities is right. It would take buckets and buckets of water."

"Buckets wouldn't do it," Johan said. "I'm thinking in terms of a pump of some sort bringing water under pressure from someplace like the river. I've read about water pressure used in gold mining to separate nuggets from the soil around them."

"But why would you want all that water pressure just to clean the barn floor?"

"Why not? The work would be done so fast, you'd

have time to take care of a dozen cows . . . maybe one hundred."

Kristin laughed. "Who'd have time to milk that many?"

"I haven't figured out that part yet," Johan said with a chuckle, "but believe me, if I don't, somebody else will."

"Someone else who shares your dream of farmland stretching out to the horizon?"

"It will be more than a dream," he said. "Wait and see."

Kristin tilted her head and studied him. "You know so many things. Where did you learn about the gold mining and the water pressure?"

"From the weekly newspaper, *The Messenger,*" he said.

"But that's a Swedish newspaper! I saw it when we stayed with the Lundgrens."

Johan's eyes twinkled with mischief. "Does news have to be written in English to make it right?"

Kristin blushed and stammered, "This—this is the United States. English is its language. The people who choose to live here should read and speak English."

"Some of them do, but it takes time to get used to new ways and new ideas. Change doesn't come quickly."

Surprised at hearing such solemn advice from Johan, Kristin teased, "You sound like such a wise old man."

"Not so old, just experienced," he said. "My father thinks my ideas about farming impractical and impossible."

"No, they're not!" Kristin cried out indignantly.

Johan beamed at her. He hefted the manure fork, ready to return to the job, but paused and said, "Next time I hear of someone from around here going to Saint Paul or Minneapolis, I'll ask them to bring you a newspaper printed in English."

Kristin didn't know which made her happier—having Johan close at hand or not having to clean the smelly barn. She fed the chickens and weeded the kitchen garden with renewed energy.

The time they had together was short because Johan had his own chores to take care of.

"Your mother told me that your father will return by tomorrow evening," Johan said to Kristin, "so I'll come back in the morning to take care of the barn."

"You don't need to," Kristin said. "I can manage it."

"I think you could manage anything," Johan answered. He tucked a finger under her chin and smiled. "But I'm coming back because I like working near you."

Kristin smiled in return and surprised herself by saying, "And I like knowing you are near."

Johan took a step forward, but at that moment Mamma opened the kitchen door and called, "Would you like to share our dinner, Johan?"

"No, thank you, Fru Swensen," he said. "I have to return to our farm and take care of my own chores."

Kristin watched him stride along the path that led down the slope and into the woods.

"Wash," Mamma said. "I'll have the food on the table by the time you've finished."

Her face and hands well scrubbed and tingling, Kristin entered the kitchen and seated herself at the table.

Mamma sat across from her and ladled a beef-and-noodle mixture into their bowls. She bowed her head and said the prayer before meals, but she had no sooner straightened in her chair than she remarked, "Johan Olsen is a fine young man."

"I suppose," Kristin said. She touched a forkful of beef to her lips, but it was very hot and she allowed it to cool.

"He seems interested in you," Mamma went on.

Kristin put down her fork. "He's only a friend, Mamma, nothing more."

"Good. You are young yet," Mamma said. "It would be well for you to wait a year, maybe two, before thinking of marriage."

"Mamma!" Kristin said. "I'm not going to marry Johan. He's a farmer."

Her mother's eyes widened. "So is your father."

"I know." Kristin paused to collect her thoughts, then spoke carefully. "Mamma, it's hard to explain what I mean, but life on a farm is very hard. It's the same old thing, over and over again, day after day. It's not like living in the city."

Mamma looked puzzled. "What could you possibly know about city life?"

Kristin shrugged. "I've been thinking about it. I want to learn more about what Sigrid—Fröken Larson is doing. I want to help work for voting rights for women. I could do that if I lived in the city."

The moment the words were out of her mouth, Kristin gave such a start of surprise that her hands trembled. Had she really been thinking that? Excitement bubbled up into her throat and she realized it was possible. It was actually possible that someday she might move to Minneapolis and get a job.

Clapping both hands to her head, Mamma said, "You don't understand what you are talking about. A proper young woman does not live alone in a strange city!"

"Fröken Larson did when she was young." Kristin was

immediately defensive. "She studied at the university, then became a teacher."

"Did Fröken Larson do this by choice? Would she admit to you that she had never been asked to marry and had no brother whose family could take her in, so there was little left for her to choose? I don't think so."

"How can you say that about her? You don't know that it's true."

"And neither do you know that what *you* believe about her is true." Mamma's chin quivered as she studied Kristin's face. "Can't you see, daughter, that a woman's greatest happiness comes from her husband and children? There is nothing more precious than new life brought into the world. A woman's family is her source of strength and love, which makes up for any and all the disappointment and worry and pain that life brings. A young woman choosing to go through life alone . . . you have no idea what you would miss."

"Maybe I could have both," Kristin said stubbornly.

"Don't wish for the whole world," Mamma answered. "Be happy with only your share of it."

Oh, Mamma, can't you see that I can't be you? Kristin thought. There was no discussing her dreams with Mamma. She'd never be able to understand.

On the Tuesday afternoon after Pappa's return Sigrid Larson rode up to the Swensens' farm in her sister's buggy. Mamma, a little wary of Fröken Larson, yet delighted to have visitors, immediately put on the coffeepot. Sigrid had brought a box of pepparkaka, and their gingery fragrance filled the parlor. "A favorite recipe from Kalmar," she said.

Sigrid seated herself on the love seat and glanced

around the room. "You have made this room beautiful," she said. "Did you weave that lovely wall hanging?"

Mamma flushed with pleasure, while Kristin hoped that from where she sat, Sigrid couldn't see some of the uneven rows. "Kristin wove it," Mamma answered. "She made the covers for two of the pillows, too. I couldn't leave them behind. I brought them all the way from Leksand."

"Oh, then you come from the Dalarna Province, where everyone seems to be artistic."

"Kristin is particularly talented."

Kristin blushed, remembering her struggle with those pillows and Mamma's concern that Kristin was having such difficulty with a task every young woman learned to do well. She was thankful when Sigrid changed the subject. She liked Sigrid, and she was happy to see that Mamma liked her, too.

Mamma chatted and laughed and poured more coffee until finally Sigrid pulled a small watch out of the pocket of her dress and said, "Oh, my! I have been having such a good time visiting with you, I had no idea it was close to four o'clock." She reached into her drawstring bag and pulled out a small book. "Here you are, Kristin," she said. "This is the book I told you about."

As Kristin took the book from Sigrid's hands, Mamma leaned forward with curiosity. "What kind of a book is this?" she asked.

"It is a book that explains the government of the United States," Sigrid told her. "I think you'd like to read it, too."

Mamma's cheeks turned pink. "I think I'll leave that to Kristin. I'm still having difficulty learning to speak the language, let alone read it."

"English is a very difficult language," Sigrid agreed. "I had a great deal of trouble at first in learning it."

"I have the same trouble." Mamma's embarrassment fled, and she sat back, taking another sip of coffee.

Kristin could hardly wait until she was alone and could open the book. "Will this tell me more about Susan B. Anthony?" she asked.

"No," Sigrid said. "Not this book. I would rather you read this first."

"Who is Susan B. Anthony?" Mamma asked.

"She is a very brave woman who has spent much of her life trying to get voting rights for women," Sigrid answered.

"Voting rights for women?" Mamma gave Kristin a pointed look and said, "I don't think that would be something we would want Kristin to read."

Kristin had her mouth open to argue, but Sigrid spoke first. "The book I've just given her simply explains the government of the United States," she said. "It's used in some of the schools in our state. Please ask your husband to look through it first if you'd like. I assure you he'll approve of Kristin's reading the book."

"Very well," Mamma said. She reached for the book, and Kristin gave it up reluctantly.

"I'd like both of you to learn more about universal suffrage," Sigrid said.

Mamma looked puzzled. "Universal suffrage? What is that?"

"Voting, Mamma," Kristin broke in. "It means *everyone* who is a citizen of the United States can vote, women as well as men."

Mamma turned to Sigrid. "Thank you, but *I* have no

wish to vote. Politics, government, laws . . . those are a man's concern, not a woman's."

"They should be a woman's, too."

"Why? Will being able to vote help me maintain a cleaner house? Bake lighter cakes? Care for my husband and daughter?"

Sigrid looked thoughtful. "Don't you see, Fru Swensen, if laws are unjust, they hurt your family. If politicians are stupid or greedy, they also hurt your family."

Mamma raised her chin stubbornly. "I told you, my husband is the one who studies the issues and protects the family through *his* vote."

Kristin expected Sigrid to best Mamma with a powerful argument, but instead she smiled and leaned back in her chair. "One of our difficulties in persuading the legislature to give women the vote is that there are many women who think as you do, Fru Swensen."

Mamma looked surprised but gratified. "And rightly so," she answered.

Sigrid stood and nodded to Mamma and to Kristin. "This has been a very pleasant afternoon for me. Thank you for your kind hospitality. *Tack för i dag!*"

"And thank you for your most enjoyable visit and for the delicious pepparkaka," Mamma said.

She bade good-bye to her guest inside the front door, but Kristin followed Sigrid out to the buggy. "Thank you for lending me the book," she said, "and no matter what Mamma said, I *do* want to read about Susan B. Anthony."

"Only with your parents' permission," Sigrid said.

"But they may not give permission," Kristin complained.

Sigrid smiled and slowly shook her head. "I hope you'll

obey your parents' wishes and try to be patient. As I told you before, change takes time."

Johan had told her the same thing, but Kristin sighed and said, "It's hard to be patient."

"Think about Susan B. Anthony. She has worked for women's rights since she was a young woman, and many women have worked with her, but we still do not have the right to vote."

"If only women like Mamma—"

"Respect your mother's opinions. You want her to respect yours."

Kristin smiled. "You're right, Sigrid. I want everything to change immediately—today if possible."

Sigrid climbed into the buggy and picked up the reins. "I've heard that Anna Shaw is coming to Minneapolis to speak. When a date is set, I'll invite both you and your mother to come visit me and hear her. In the meantime I'll see you at Midsommarfest."

It would be no use, Kristin thought, sick with disappointment. Not only would Mamma never agree to go to the lecture in Minneapolis with her, but Pappa would refuse to allow either of them to go. She watched the buggy until it was out of sight, then hurried into the house to help Mamma with preparations for dinner.

It was during the meal that Mamma told Pappa about Sigrid Larson's visit. A scowl darkened his face, and as though Kristin were not with them at the table, he said, "We do not want Kristin associating with this Fröken Larson. I have been told about her. She is a great embarrassment to her sister, Fru Dalquist, because of her outlandish ideas about men and women, and Kristin seems overly receptive to ideas of this sort."

"Pappa," Kristin tried to explain, but he raised a hand, palm out, a signal to be silent.

"There is no room for discussion," he said.

"You *used* to discuss things with me."

"You see," Mamma broke in. "When she was young, you gave her too much freedom. I told you at the time that nothing good would come of it."

Pappa shrugged and frowned. "A few fishing trips, working together with the animals . . ."

"From the beginning she should have been raised as a daughter, not as a son."

"What's done is done," Pappa said. He turned to Kristin. "Nothing more will be said about Fröken Larson in this house."

"But the book about government . . ."

"When I have time, I will read the book and decide if it is appropriate reading for you."

Kristin stared at her plate, too angry to eat. Pappa might stop her now, but he couldn't stop her forever. *Just wait, Pappa!* she thought. *I'll show you what I can do!*

CHAPTER NINE

❖ ❖ ❖

KRISTIN was still angry as she finished washing the dishes. She hung the damp towels over a rack to dry, then slipped out the kitchen door, striding down the path to the lake. The sky was still light, a silvered blue that shimmered over long, bright evenings.

She walked down to the shore, hugging her arms and thinking how unfair her father had been. She wanted to read the book Sigrid had brought her! She had a right to!

A twig snapped in the forest behind Kristin, startling her. As a branch scraped softly against another branch, she whirled around, her heart pounding, and demanded, "Who's there?"

"I didn't mean to scare you," Johan said as he pushed aside a tree limb and stepped out of the woods. He pulled a fishing pole free, examining it carefully.

"Fishing in the woods?" Kristin could hear the remnants of fear still in her voice and she tried to cover it with a joke. "Have the bass and muskie taken to the trees?"

"They may have, because I've been fishing along the west shore and haven't been able to find them." Johan gave a wave of one hand toward the promontory behind him, adding, "I didn't want to get my feet wet, so I cut across the land. This cove is a pretty good place to fish."

"Do you come here often?"

"Often enough," he said. "So do a couple of my friends. I know this is your father's land, but we've used this spot for years. I hope he doesn't mind."

Kristin, remembering her dip in the pool, turned warm from the top of her head to her toes. There was no question about it—she had lost her right to enjoy cooling off in the lake. She had no rights—not even the right to read a book about something as innocent as a country's government. A woman had no rights at all.

"Johan," Kristin blurted out, "that Methodist singing school you told me about . . . I want to go."

He raised his head, surprised. "When we talked about it, I thought you were teasing."

"I was then . . . a little, but there's no reason why we shouldn't go. You said they meet every Wednesday evening, didn't you?"

"Yes." The word was drawn out, reluctant.

"Then take me to the singing school. Please?"

"Kristin, I told you our pastor doesn't approve."

"What does that matter? The Methodists aren't going to harm us." When Johan didn't answer immediately, she said in challenge, "Are you afraid of what will happen if we should get caught?"

Johan hesitated for just an instant before he replied, "You're not afraid of anything, are you, Kristin?"

When Kristin didn't answer, Johan asked, "What will your parents say?"

"I won't ask them," she answered, and wished the sudden uncomfortable feeling in the pit of her stomach would go away. "I'll just tell them that I'm going for a ride with you."

"All right, Kristin," Johan said. "If you really want to go, I'll come for you around six-thirty."

As he walked off, following the path around the lake, Kristin heard him mumble, "There's nothing wrong with singing. And going to another church to sing—not to pray of course—well, what's the harm in that?"

Thoroughly miserable and wishing tomorrow night would never come, Kristin slapped away the mosquitoes that had gathered in the damp night air and hurried up the path to her house.

Pappa left early Wednesday morning with the promise to return by Saturday evening. It wasn't until supper was finished that Kristin told her mother she'd be going out riding with Johan to visit some friends. Embarrassed by the knowing look on her mother's face, Kristin wanted to insist, *You're wrong—it isn't like that,* but she couldn't say anything at all.

In her room she washed her face, neck, and upper body with the cool water she poured into the china bowl, then dressed in the plain, dark brown dress she usually wore to church on Sundays. She wished she didn't have to go to the singing school. Oh, how much she wished she didn't have to go! But when she heard Johan's knock on the door, her heartbeat quickened, and she hurried down the stairs to meet him.

"I'll bring Kristin home between nine-thirty and ten o'clock," Johan told Mamma.

Kristin, unable to meet her mother's eyes, turned and

followed Johan to his father's buggy, allowing him to help her inside and drive out to the road before she said a word.

"If you've changed your mind . . ." she murmured.

"I haven't," he said, and turned to look at her. "Have you?"

Kristin gulped. "No."

"If you're afraid—"

"I am *not* afraid." Kristin sat up a little straighter and stared directly ahead.

On the way to the church Johan talked about family members Kristin hadn't met. He had two cousins and an uncle who worked in the lumber mills during the winter months. Kristin didn't tell him this was her father's plan, too. It was too difficult to talk.

When they arrived at the Methodist church meeting room, however, her mood changed. Johan introduced her to Will, his friend, and Will saw to it that Kristin met everyone in the group.

"Do you know many of the latest songs?" Will asked.

Kristin giggled. "I know the words to 'Yankee Doodle.' I learned it on the ship coming to America."

A plump girl, as blond as Jenny, handed Kristin a song sheet and said, "That song is as old as the United States itself. People sang it during the Revolutionary War. We can teach you songs everyone's singing today."

Kristin was delighted to see that most of the songs on the sheet were written in English.

A tall, long-legged boy had brought a fiddle, and a small, shy girl named Alice took charge of the piano.

Will, who was the song leader, announced, "Let's start with 'In the Good Old Summertime,' " and Kristin turned to smile at Johan, whispering, "Won't they be surprised that you know the words?"

Johan smiled back, and Kristin was glad to see he was already enjoying himself. She joined in the singing with enthusiasm.

A few hymns were sung. They were unfamiliar to Kristin, but she sat with the others, smothering an uncomfortable guilt that she was participating in prayer that wasn't strictly Lutheran and glad that Pastor Holcomb would never know.

Kristin was surprised when nine o'clock arrived and the singing school was over.

"Come back next week," people called to her as she left with Johan.

"Do you want to?" he asked as he took the reins and guided the horses to the roadway.

She looked up at him. "You'd bring me here if I said yes, wouldn't you?"

Johan nodded, and Kristin, still filled with the fun and the friendship of the evening, reached over and placed a hand over his. "Thank you," she murmured. "I had a wonderful time, but tonight was enough."

"I understand," he said. "You had to prove to yourself you could do it."

Indignantly Kristin pulled back her hand. "I was not trying to prove anything to myself!"

"Yes, you were. And this wasn't the first time."

"If you're referring to my Sunday-school class—"

"That was just part of it."

"The men's clothes—that's what you're talking about, isn't it? They were the only things I could put on. And the lake—"

"What about the lake?"

"Nothing," Kristin said quickly. "What I mean is, I'm not trying to prove anything to myself. I just want to be able to do all the things that men do."

"I can accept that," Johan said.

Kristin's mouth dropped open, and it took her a moment to collect her thoughts. "Do you mean you think that women should have the same rights men do?"

"I guess I do," Johan answered, "because I can't think of a good reason why they shouldn't." He glanced at Kristin and smiled. "It's getting cool. Aren't you chilly sitting way over there?"

Kristin slid toward Johan, moving close as he put an arm around her shoulders. "You wouldn't object if women won the right to vote?"

"Not if that's what they want."

Encouraged, Kristin said, "Someday I'm going to go to Minneapolis and work for women's suffrage."

Johan chuckled. "That's fine," he said, "if you haven't got anything better to do."

Kristin sighed. Johan didn't understand, after all, but at least his attitude was better than Pappa's. The night was cool, but Johan's arm was warm, and his shoulder was strong. She snuggled even closer.

How Pastor Holcomb found out, Kristin couldn't imagine. Although he didn't mention her by name, he thundered from the pulpit about the dangers of attending activities organized by the Methodists. "It is more than simply taking part in such frivolities," he said. "It's important that our young people not dilute the Lutheran church in America by associations that could lead to marriage with those of other faiths." .

"I am considering the fact," he added with a quick

scowl in Kristin's direction, "that one of our two young people who attended the Methodist singing school could possibly be unaware of our ways, but there will be no excuse in the future for involving herself or others in detrimental pursuits."

There was a rustle in the pew behind Kristin, and she heard Clara whisper her name. Of course everyone would know who Pastor Holcomb was talking about, just as everyone seemed to know about her Sunday-school disaster. Kristin squirmed in her seat, wishing she could slide under the pew and disappear.

Mamma sat stiffly beside her, staring straight ahead, and Kristin imagined that she and Pappa would have a great deal to discuss with her once they were on the way home.

Directly after services, however, Jenny and some of the girls Kristin had met clustered around her.

"You didn't!" Jenny squealed with delight.

"Who went with you?" Minnie asked.

Jenny nudged Ida with an elbow. "Johan Olsen. Isn't that obvious, the way he looks at her?"

Kristin stared down at her toes. "I'm sorry it happened. It was all my fault. I didn't think Johan and I would get into trouble. I didn't think Pastor Holcomb would find out."

Josie spoke with an older, superior attitude. "What it comes down to is that you didn't think at all."

Fru Berglund joined the group, clapping a hand on her daughter's shoulder as she glanced at Kristin with disapproval. "Jenny," she said, "will you come with me, please? I could use your help in getting our food on the table."

The twins' mother called to them, and the other girls—

expecting the same from their mothers—left Kristin. She hurried to join her parents, realizing too late that they were in conversation with Johan and his parents. The conversation broke off abruptly as they saw Kristin.

Her face burning with embarrassment, Kristin quickly said, "The blame is all mine, and I'm sorry, Fru Olsen, Herr Olsen. I asked Johan to take me to the singing school. I didn't mean to get him into trouble."

To her surprise Herr Olsen smiled. "Don't be distressed, Kristin, and don't take the blame on yourself. The responsibility lies with Johan. It's up to a young man to know what is proper or improper to do."

"I *asked* him to take me. He was only trying to please me."

"I imagine he was." Kristin couldn't believe it when Herr Olsen chuckled and glanced at her father. At least not everyone in the parish disapproved of what she had done.

Pappa said, "You and Johan have both apologized to us, and once you have made your peace with Pastor Holcomb, the episode need not be referred to again."

"And it will not be repeated," Mamma said quietly. The look she gave Kristin was one that meant business.

Herr Olsen patted his stomach. "Enough of this talk," he said. "I, for one, am hungry. Why don't the Swensens join the Olsen family and share a meal?"

Fru Olsen and Mamma began to open baskets, shake out tablecloths, and set out the platters and bowls they had brought, while their husbands stood to one side, watching in anticipation.

As the younger Olsen children ran past them to the table, Kristin looked up at Johan and whispered, "I was wrong. I shouldn't have involved you, and I'm sorry."

He smiled. "My only problem is that some of my friends are jealous of me. Besides being an exciting girl, you're very pretty, Kristin."

She brushed off the compliment with a quick shake of her head. "I'm also an outcast," she said.

"You won't be for long. It's just the mothers' way of teaching their daughters a lesson. People like you. They just don't approve of what you did. You'll find they're quick to forgive and forget."

Resentment stung like the prick of a needle. Kristin said, "I did nothing to any of them. There's nothing to forgive." She turned so that her back was to the Berglund family, seated at a table a short distance away. "Besides, it makes no difference what any of them thinks of me. I don't care."

She hoped Johan couldn't see in her face how much she really did care.

There was no meeting scheduled for the Young People's Society, so Kristin played with the youngest Olsen child—two-year-old Tilde—who finally fell asleep on Kristin's lap. Tilde was warm and snuggly, and as Kristin held her close, she wondered what it would have been like to grow up with brothers or sisters. For the first time she allowed herself to think about the babies Mamma had lost. They would have been her older brothers—tall and strong like Johan. She had never known them, had never even known *about* them until now. For an instant the full realization of their loss was almost too painful to bear.

Fru Olsen broke into Kristin's thoughts by sending Johan to find Carl, his twelve-year-old brother. "Whenever that boy is out of sight, I know he's getting into mischief," Fru Olsen scolded, but Kristin could hear the love and pride in her voice.

Fru Olsen, Mamma, Fru Berglund—they reminded Kristin of the barnyard hens scurrying to throw protective wings over their chicks.

She smiled, and Fru Olsen appraised her with sharp eyes. "Kristin," she said, "do you like to do needlework?"

Kristin hesitated, then tried to avoid a direct answer. "From the time Mamma taught me, she demanded only the tiniest of stitches."

"It is good to be a skilled seamstress," Fru Olsen said. She pointed to the empty bowls on the table. "I hope you're also as good a cook as your mother is."

Kristin knew her answer would sound as though she were being modest, but unfortunately it was the truth. "I could never be as good a cook as Mamma is. I can only copy her wonderful recipes."

Fru Olsen nodded, apparently pleased with Kristin's answer. Two of her children ran to her, tugging at her sleeves and noisily demanding she settle a squabble. By the time she had scolded them both and rendered a firm decision, Mamma had changed the subject to the Midsommarfest, and the two women were off on this interesting subject.

Kristin was glad to have escaped any further questioning. Maybe she could be a better cook if she really tried, but did she have to be—just because she was a woman?

CHAPTER TEN

❖ ❖ ❖

ALTHOUGH Pappa was filled with good spirits on the ride home, Mamma was quiet, and from the moment she entered the house and changed from her church clothes to a simple cotton dress, she bustled about the kitchen, banging pots and pans as though she were angry.

"I've really upset Mamma," Kristin told her father. "I'd better talk to her and tell her how sorry I am."

Pappa smiled as though he knew a secret joke. "Why don't you go for a little walk?" he asked. "Mamma and I need to talk."

Worried, Kristin asked, "Is everything all right?"

"Even better than all right," Pappa answered. "Now, run along, Kristin. I want to talk to your mother."

Kristin strolled down to the lake, breathing in the fragrance of sun-soaked grass, the sweet-sharpness of clover in bloom, and the perfume of tart wild strawberries, which were tucked under scraggly leaves in the shady, sandy patches near the path. The lake lay still in the warm, sluggish air, with barely a ripple to break its surface. The cove was a silent, lonely place, and Kristin wished she had someone to talk to—Jenny, maybe, or Johan. She didn't like feeling so left out, so terribly alone.

She waited at least a half hour before returning home and entered the kitchen door timidly calling, "Hello?"

"We're in the parlor," Mamma called in return, and Kristin was relieved to hear the usual no-nonsense strength in Mamma's voice.

Kristin found her parents looking through a box of papers and photographs.

"Our wedding picture," Pappa said, and handed it to Kristin.

She had seen it before. Her parents, looking very young, were seated at least two feet apart on straight-backed kitchen chairs on the lawn in front of *Mormor*'s house. Mamma wore a small, round hat perched on top of her head and a high-necked, long-sleeved dark dress with a tiny pinched-in waist and ruffles around the hem of the skirt. Pappa looked uncomfortable in a stiff collar and a dark wool suit. Neither of them smiled as they held very still for the camera's long exposure, but they both had pleased expressions on their faces.

"That was a very happy day," Pappa said. "I won the most beautiful girl in Dalarna Province for my wife."

Mamma chuckled. "It was a happy day for both of us. I have always been glad that my parents arranged our betrothal."

"Always?" Kristin asked. "Even when you had dis-agreements or when Pappa decided to do something you didn't want to do, like coming to America, or—"

"Always," Mamma repeated. "Disagreements can be settled, problems can be worked out. Two people caring

about each other enough to go through life together—
that is what brings happiness."

"And children that come from a marriage," Pappa
added. "Children bring happiness."

Kristin thought of the soft, warm bundle called Tilde
Olsen, and she smiled. "I guess they do," she said.

"You and I, Kristin," Mamma said, "are going to make
up for a great deal of lost time. There is no reason why
you shouldn't be able to make cakes as light as any in
Great Rock Lake. And with practice your weaving and
embroidery can improve. You can make up your mind
to learn, can't you?"

So that's why Mamma had been upset, Kristin thought.
She'd been embarrassed by Kristin's half-truths to Fru
Olsen. "Yes, Mamma," Kristin murmured reluctantly.
"I'll try."

Mamma suddenly took the picture from Kristin, put it
back inside the box, and stood up. "There's too much to
do to just sit here all evening," she said. "It's time for
the cows to be brought back and milked, the vegetables
to be added to the broth, and tomorrow's bread to be
set out to rise."

Kristin was reluctant to intrude on her parents' close-
ness. "Let me bring in the cows and milk them, Pappa,"
she said. "It will take me only a few minutes to change
my dress and shoes."

He smiled and nodded indulgently. *Pappa must be
earning more money than he thought he would,* Kristin
decided. *Why else would he be in such a happy mood?*

The next afternoon Jenny came to visit, riding sidesad-
dle on a lumpy-shouldered, sway-backed horse, and

found Kristin hunting for eggs in the henhouse, which had been built at one side of the barn.

"Want me to help you search for hidden nests?" she asked Kristin.

"I've already spotted a couple," Kristin said, "but the hens are setting on them, and we're hoping the chicks will hatch." She shifted the bowl holding eggs to one hip and said, "Tether your horse and come into the house. Would you like coffee? Cold buttermilk?"

"Buttermilk, thanks." As Jenny fastened the reins of her horse to a post outside the barn door, she said, "I told my mother I wanted to come and visit you. I convinced her that it took a little while for a newcomer to get used to our ways and you'd soon settle down." She grinned. "But I hope you don't. I like you the way you are."

Warm with gratitude, Kristin said, "You're probably the only person in Great Rock Lake who does."

Jenny laughed. "That's not the way I heard it." Before Kristin had a chance to answer, she said, "Tell me, what did Pastor Holcomb say when you and Johan gave him your apology? Did you look properly humble and repentant? Did he scowl down his nose and give you one of his fearsome looks? He used to scare me to death when I was little."

Kristin laughed and led Jenny into the kitchen, where Mamma greeted her warmly. She placed glasses of buttermilk and crisp cinnamon-sugared rusks on the table for them to share before she left the room.

Jenny immediately noticed the Dala-horse. "I have one exactly like that—even the same size," she said. "My aunt sent it to me from Dalarna."

Kristin lovingly ran one fingertip down the decorated

mane of her horse. "My grandmother gave this to me when we last said good-bye. I'll always treasure it because it was hers when she was a little girl, and because she gave it to me with so much love."

"Are you still as homesick as you were?" Jenny asked.

Kristin thought about it. "Not as much," she answered, "but there are moments."

"Having friends helps," Jenny said matter-of-factly, and went on to tell Kristin something funny Clara had done.

They ate and chatted and laughed for more than an hour, and when it was time for Jenny to leave, Kristin was sorry to see her go.

"Come to our farm and visit me next," Jenny said.

"I don't know if I can," Kristin told her. "We have only the one horse, and when Pappa takes the wagon on a hauling job, we have no transportation at all."

Jenny wasn't fazed. "Then I'll come here again, but not until after Midsommarfest. I'll have to help Mamma get everything ready for it."

Kristin knew how much preparation went into the festival. It was one of the most important days of the year. "What kind of games will there be for the people our age at your Midsommarfest?" she asked.

"At *our* Midsommarfest. You live here, too," Jenny reminded her. She laughed at Kristin's embarrassment and said, "Lots of circle games like 'Skip to My Lou' and 'Jolly Is the Miller' and *'Tre Glada Gossar i en Ring,'* and then everything ends with a Grand March." Her eyes sparkling, Jenny said, "I'm hoping Paul will ask me to be his partner in the Grand March, and I know who you'll want to ask you."

Kristin laughed, and she began to be excited about joining in the celebration.

That afternoon and the next, Pappa and Herr Olsen met down by the lake path, and on both occasions Pappa didn't return home until it was time for the cows to be brought back from pasture. "We've been discussing property," Pappa explained with a smile. Kristin guessed that if Pappa was thinking of acquiring even more land, things must be looking up.

Although Mamma still kept a watchful eye out for unwelcome spirits, she also seemed happier than in recently past days.

On Friday morning Pappa made an announcement that made Kristin happy as well: The Olsen family would be coming that evening for dessert and coffee.

Kristin's heart jumped. She hadn't seen Johan since Sunday, and she missed him.

"Perhaps," Mamma said, "we should bake something special for the occasion. Cookies would be nice for the children. *Sandbakelser* and *spritz,* or maybe butter rings with vanilla sugar."

"Do we have dry cocoa?" Kristin asked. "You could . . ." She looked at the expression on Mamma's face and quickly added, "That is, I guess that *I* could bake a chocolate roll."

"Fine," Pappa said. "Nothing tastes better than a chocolate roll with cream filling."

"I just thought of something," Kristin said. "This is the first time since we moved to Great Rock Lake that we've invited guests to our home."

"Then it's an occasion worth remembering," Pappa said, his eyes twinkling.

CHAPTER ELEVEN

✦ ✦ ✦

KRISTIN washed her hands and began the baking preparations, working side by side with her mother. The kitchen soon filled with the mingled fragrances of cinnamon, sugar, vanilla, and chocolate; and Kristin was pleased with the array of cookies and cakes. The work hadn't been that hard, and she couldn't wait to eat all the good food.

She picked up a strip of the buttery-thin *spritz* and popped it into her mouth. "Perfect," she told her mother. "The Olsen children are going to love these cookies."

Mamma handed Kristin a rag. "Polish the furniture— every inch of it. I want Fru Olsen to see that our house is every bit as clean as hers is."

"How do we know how clean hers is?"

"Never mind," Mamma said. "Just do it."

Kristin's mother was a hard taskmaster. With the extra cleaning to do in addition to her regular chores, Kristin was exhausted. Why did this have to be such a major event? she wondered. They had entertained Sigrid Larson without all the fuss and had had a very good time, and Kristin's visit with Jenny in the kitchen had been the most fun of all. "When I have a house of my own," she said, "I'm going to entertain company without so much bother."

Mamma looked at her sharply. "That remains to be seen," she said. "Now, hurry upstairs and get ready. Your brown dress will be nice. If you like, I'll rebraid your hair."

For years Kristin had competently managed the long, flaxen braid that hung down her back, so she was surprised and touched by Mamma's offer. Her mother was sparing with loving words and hugs, but Kristin recognized her love in many other ways.

Finally all was ready. On every gleaming surface bowls of blue spiderwort, with their spiky leaves, mingled with shafts of pink-and-white lady's slipper; and the parlor lamps sparkled with light, in spite of the long, sun-drenched twilight.

Soon the Olsens arrived, and Kristin was delighted when Tilde ran to her, holding up her arms to be picked up.

Greetings were hearty and overloud, and to Kristin's surprise even Johan seemed nervous. But Tilde demanded Kristin's complete attention, so any questions she might have had were soon out of mind.

The children were fed milk and cookies in the kitchen, and as soon as they were settled, the adults congregated in the parlor.

"I'll stay with the children," Kristin said. "When they've finished eating, I can take them out to the meadow to play."

"No, Kristin," Mamma said. "I want you to come with us."

After taking her Dala-horse to the parlor, out of the reach of the children, Kristin dutifully helped her mother serve steaming cups of coffee and slices of chocolate roll, which were exclaimed over, praised, and enjoyed.

"Kristin made the cake," Mamma said proudly.

And Fru Olsen remarked, "I must have the recipe. This cake is even lighter than my own."

"I added two extra egg whites to the batter and used the yolks in the cream filling," Kristin said. She cringed as she heard herself sounding so much like Mamma and her housewife friends.

Pappa put down his coffee cup and turned to Herr Olsen. "This is a good time to tell Kristin and Johan about our pact," he said.

"What pact?" Kristin asked. She looked from face to face.

No one answered her. Herr Olsen nodded and beamed at everyone in the room as he said, "In less than a year and a half Johan will be twenty-one, old enough to have his own farm and establish his own family. I am giving him the good pastureland and fields between our farm and the Swensen farm."

"And I am adding to it a fine section of lakeshore land," Pappa said. His smile grew broader. "This land will be presented to Johan and Kristin soon after her eighteenth birthday when they marry."

"What!" Kristin dropped her cup, coffee splashing across her skirt. "What do you mean, 'when they marry'?"

"It should be a happy surprise for you, daughter,"

Pappa said. "We've been well aware of your interest in this fine young man and his interest in you."

"We've agreed on a prenuptial arrangement," Herr Olsen told her. "Both mothers think the two of you are still too young for marriage, which is why we have set the date for a little over a year from now."

"But you can't!" Kristin said. Everyone stared at her, but she was so stunned, she didn't care.

Bewildered, Pappa said, "Kristin, this is good land—the best."

Kristin got to her feet, although her legs were so weak, she wondered if they'd hold her up. "You're trading me for a piece of land? You can't! This is the United States, not Sweden. In this country I should have the freedom to make up my own mind. I should be able to choose the husband I want when I want and *if* I want!"

"Kristin! Think about what you are saying!" Mamma's face was white.

Startled by the look of horror in her mother's eyes, Kristin tried to calm down. There were manners to remember, polite things to be said. But how could she? They had no right to do this to her!

She glanced toward Johan, who sat bent over, staring at the floor, his forearms resting on his thighs, and Kristin felt as though she'd been hit in the stomach. "Oh, Johan," she cried, "I didn't mean to hurt you. I like you very much. We're friends, and I want us to stay friends. You understand, don't you?"

Johan didn't answer. He didn't even look up. The two sets of parents sat like statues, unable to speak or move.

Gulping a long breath to steady herself, Kristin tried to explain. "I don't mind the hard work of running a farm. I'm used to it. I've lived on a farm all my life. But

I don't want to spend the rest of my life doing what I've always done. I want to go to the city. I want to get a job in Minneapolis."

Fru Olsen was the first to speak. "What kind of a girl are you?" she asked. "A proper young woman doesn't travel by herself to a city and live there alone. It's not right. It's not even safe."

"Fröken Larson—"

"We are not discussing Fröken Larson and her nonconforming ways. We are discussing you." She carefully put down her cup and got to her feet. "You are a foolish girl for rejecting my son and all that his family offers."

"I'm not rejecting Johan. I—I like Johan."

Before she sailed toward the kitchen, Fru Olsen said to her husband, "Bring the buggy around. I'll get the children."

Mamma jumped to her feet and ran after Fru Olsen. "Don't be angry," she begged. "This is *our* fault. Knowing how independent Kristin has always been, we should have prepared her. But I thought she cared for Johan. I thought she'd be as pleased as I was when my father arranged my marriage. I remember my own surprise and joy—"

Fru Olsen spoke loudly enough for her voice to carry back to Kristin. "We were willing to overlook your daughter's misbehavior because we believed she would outgrow her young, willful ways and because Johan wanted her for his wife. But there are many other, better-behaved young women in this part of Minnesota. He can look elsewhere and have a happier marriage as a result."

Without a word Herr Olsen strode through the front door, and Pappa followed him, shutting the door loudly as he left.

Kristin dropped to her knees in front of Johan and tried to take his hands, but he didn't respond. "I thought you understood what I wanted to do," she cried. "You told me you believed that women should have the same rights as men. You told me!"

For the first time he raised his head and looked into Kristin's eyes. Johan's own eyes were so dark and deep with pain that Kristin shuddered. "If you wanted to go to meetings and work for women's right to vote, I would have let you," he said, "because you'd be supporting something you believed in, and I would never try to stand between you and your beliefs. But there are other parts of life, Kristin. I would have loved you. I would have been a good husband to you and a good father to our children."

He pulled his hands away from hers and got to his feet, sidestepping around her.

"Johan!" Kristin cried. Tears burned her cheeks, and she tried to brush them away with the back of one hand. "Why didn't you tell me how you felt about me? Why didn't you come to me yourself?"

But Johan didn't answer. He left the parlor, following the direction his father had taken.

Kristin reached for her Dala-horse and hugged it closely as she pillowed her head on the chair, the upholstery still warm from Johan's body. She heard the Olsens leave, and in a short while her parents reentered the house.

Pappa didn't say a word. He stomped up the stairs to his bedroom, but Mamma dropped into the nearest parlor chair and wiped her reddened eyes with a handkerchief she'd pulled from her sleeve.

Her voice was heavy with tears as she said, "Even in

rural Sweden some girls resist family custom and want to choose the men they marry. I can understand this. But here in the United States, we are struggling to exist. Herr Olsen is a prosperous farmer who could be a big help to your father, and Johan is as fine a young man as you're ever likely to meet."

"I know he is," Kristin answered, "but I don't love him."

"You gave us the impression that you like him."

"I *do* like him. I like him very much, but that's the difference. I like him. I don't love him."

"Of course you don't. Not yet. Love isn't a fragile buttercup whose petals open overnight. Love grows as you learn more about each other and care more about each other. It becomes richer and deeper as you share both happiness and problems together."

"Mamma, you can't say that every marriage is like that."

"No," Mamma said. She blew her nose loudly before she could continue. "But our marriage is, and we believed that your marriage to Johan could be just as happy. Your father and I want only happiness for you. A young woman should have a husband to take care of her."

"Mamma! I can take care of myself!"

"So you think, but you know nothing about what life is like for a spinster—especially one without brothers who could care for her. I was afraid you had little opportunity to make a good marriage in Leksand, and I hoped that in a new country, in a new place—"

Kristin interrupted. "You told me yourself I was too young to marry."

"You are, for now, but the agreement was for a marriage after you are eighteen."

"Pappa talked you into it. You'd agree with anything he'd say."

"Your father is the head of our family. I respect his opinions."

Kristin groaned. "And you don't understand *my* opinions."

"Apparently not," Mamma said. "And there is something else I don't understand. Where are you going to get the money to travel to Minneapolis to live? And once you're there, how are you going to earn enough money to support yourself?"

"I don't know," Kristin said honestly. She didn't have a cent of her own. Kristin wouldn't even be able to pay the train fare to get to Minneapolis to hear Anna Shaw's lecture. Independence carried a price. What was she going to do?

CHAPTER TWELVE

❖ ❖ ❖

SATURDAY Kristin begged her parents to stay home and miss the Midsommarfest.

"There is nothing I would like better to do," Pappa said, "but on Sundays we have always gone to church. Tomorrow we will also go to church."

At least he was speaking to her. All morning he had avoided her as much as possible. Mamma had mumbled references to the *spöken* who had brought them such bad luck, and breakfast had been a miserable, silent affair.

"Then could we just go to church and leave immediately after?" Kristin asked.

Mamma, who was busy sliding pans of bread from the oven, spoke up. "Do you think you can hide from everyone in Great Rock Lake? Perhaps Fru Olsen kept her thoughts and feelings about you to herself. We don't know. But whether the people in the community know or not, we must go about our business as though nothing has happened."

Kristin shuddered, well aware of how the smallest bit

of gossip grew and spread in rural areas, where anything the slightest bit out of the ordinary became intensely interesting news.

Mamma continued, "We have no choice. We must put in an appearance at Midsommarfest and behave with as much good grace as possible."

"If you and Pappa want to go, that's fine," Kristin said, "but I'd like to stay home."

"No," Pappa said. "You will come with us."

"Why can't I make this decision for myself?"

"Because you are a child."

"I'm seventeen. I'm *not* a child."

"You have behaved like a child—a very spoiled and rude child."

"Because I want to think for myself?"

He ignored her question and announced, "We will all go to the Midsommarfest. We'll put on brave faces and do our best to add to the enjoyment of the day."

Kristin clutched at his sleeve. "Please, Pappa . . . I don't want to see Johan and his family. Not now. Not yet." She could see the pain in his eyes as they met hers, and guilt made her feel ill. "I didn't mean to hurt them or hurt you and Mamma. If only you hadn't tried to surprise me. . . ."

"I was following the tradition of finding a suitable husband for you. I expected you to respect my good judgment."

"As I did, and my mother before me, and her mother before her," Mamma put in.

"That was in *Sweden*," Kristin protested. "The United States is different. Here there are more choices, more ways of doing things."

Neither parent answered her. Mamma simply said,

"Come, Kristin. Help me by washing the strawberries for the Ost-Kaka."

Early Sunday morning, as soon as the animals had been cared for and a light breakfast eaten, Kristin and her parents dressed in the bright festival costumes they had brought from Sweden.

Pappa wore dark blue knee britches and a sleeveless, striped blue-and-green vest that buttoned to the collar with two rows of gold buttons. The sleeves of his white shirt were full, caught into snug cuffs at the wrist, and his collar was stiff and pointed. Polished black shoes, knit white stockings, and a flat blue velvet cap completed his costume.

Mamma's skirt was black, and her long-sleeved, crisply ironed shirt and apron were white, but the scarf over her shoulders, pinned in front with a small gold circle, was bright red, as were her small cap and her hose.

Kristin waited for the routine that always followed. Mamma would tell Pappa how handsome he looked; then she'd twirl and prance past him, a coquettish look in her eyes, while he'd remark that she was the most beautiful woman in Leksand.

But they were no longer in Leksand. They were in the United States, and things were different in the United States, no matter how hard the people here clung to the ways they'd known in Sweden.

Kristin's parents didn't tease or compliment each other, and neither of them gave their usual enthusiastic approval to her navy-blue skirt with the red piping at the hem and the red vest she wore over her white shirt. Instead they solemnly loaded the wagon with the food they'd be taking to the Midsommarfest. "Bring the jar of strawberries and hurry," Mamma said to Kristin. "We don't want to be late."

When they arrived at the church, which was draped in garlands of green foliage, Kristin could see a maypole rising from the meadow. She loved to join in the maypole folk dance, holding a bright ribbon, twisting in and out among the other dancers to make a pattern down the pole. Today . . . no. Today, as far as she was concerned, there would be no maypole.

As Kristin walked into the church behind her mother, she felt that every eye was on her. She had planned to stay calm and detached, but she couldn't, and the blush that burned her cheeks gave her away.

Pastor Holcomb's sermon was mercifully short, which suited Kristin, because no matter how hard she tried, she couldn't keep her mind on what he was saying. In less than an hour and a half church services were over, and the younger children raced toward the meadow where the games would be held.

The countryside was much like that in Sweden, the bandstand, the church, the games area—they were all the same—but the people, who had arrived in great numbers, were not. The festival costumes in the Dalarna Province had always been much the same, but the people in Great Rock Lake had come from many parts of Sweden, and their clothing was surprisingly different.

Mrs. Lundgren, plump and happy, wore a plain white shirt and apron over a flowered skirt that stopped at least four inches above her ankles to show stockings as bright blue as the shawl around her shoulders. Josie's red-and-green apron was topped with a laced red corset around her midriff, and she wore a garland of flowers around her head. Fru Dalquist was dressed somberly in black and white, with a pale tan-striped apron and shawl, but her husband was resplendent in a bright red vest worn over his full-sleeved shirt and dark blue knee pants. Thick white stockings, a striped string tie, and a navy-blue beret completed his costume. Most of the women wore caps— either small and flowered or tidy and lacy. Only a few had bedecked themselves with flower circlets instead.

The colors of the costumes were vibrant and cheerful, but Kristin felt anything but cheerful. She should have realized that Midsommarfest in the United States would not be like the Midsommarfest she had always known in which her neighbors and friends dressed much the same, the celebration was regional, and the gold of the summer sky ceased for only the held breath of a moment.

Kristin, standing close by her mother, who was talking with Fru Dalquist, searched the crowd for Johan. Although his parents were on hand, in conversation with Pastor Holcomb, Johan was nowhere in sight.

Feeling worse by the minute and needing a friend to talk to, Kristin looked for Jenny and finally saw her across the way with her parents. Jenny glanced over, caught Kristin's eye, and sent her a quick, surreptitious wave before turning back to her parents.

Jenny knows, Kristin thought with a sick feeling in the pit of her stomach. If Jenny knew, then it must be common knowledge in the community of Great Rock Lake that Kristin had refused a prenuptial agreement with Johan. What had she done to Johan? And to his parents and hers?

Angrily she thought, *It's not all my fault. What did my parents do to me?*

The games for the younger children began, and Kristin

had to smile, in spite of the way she felt, at the tangle of boys who tried to hurry too fast in the three-legged race.

Six musicians filed into the small bandstand and tuned up their instruments. Besides the usual band instruments, one of the men held a Swedish *nyckelharpa*. Bowed like a violin, its strings were shortened by keys rather than by fingers. Kristin was eager for the music to begin. Maybe it would distract her from the misery that was causing a hard, undissolvable knot in her stomach.

The program of folk music began with a lively tune for children, *"Ro, Ro till Fiskeskär."* As some of the young ones sang along in Swedish, Kristin mentally translated the words into English: "Row, row to the fishing rocks."

The song brought back bittersweet memories of when she was twelve and snippy Mai Holder had sung it loudly, taunting Kristin in front of her classmates for acting like a rowdy boy instead of a proper girl. She had rubbed Mai's face into the dust, knowing there would be scoldings and discipline from both her teacher and her parents, but she didn't care. Hearing Mai squawl as she spit dirt from her mouth was worth whatever punishment came next.

Bountiful platters and bowls of food were set up on long trencher tables, and Kristin was called to help her mother and some of the other women serve. The church had been packed with visitors from other areas, and they enthusiastically sampled the dishes the women of Great Rock Lake had made. The people she knew who passed through the serving line smiled and spoke politely to Kristin, but she could sense their reserve.

The most difficult moment arrived when Herr and Fru Olsen came through the line with their children. As

Mamma forked slices of spiced ham onto their plates, Kristin adding spoonsful of boiled parsley potatoes, she couldn't keep from asking Fru Olsen, "Where is Johan?"

Fru Olsen stopped in the middle of separating Carl and Arnold, who were snatching from each other's plate, and answered briefly, "He wouldn't come." She hurried down the line, herding her children with her.

Soon Jenny and her parents came through the line. Jenny waited until her mother was busy scolding her father for taking too many meatballs and whispered to Kristin, "I have to talk to you. Meet me in the graveyard after dinner."

What an appropriate place, Kristin thought wryly. She needed a graveyard for her dreams.

Mamma put a hand on Kristin's shoulder and gave it a friendly squeeze. "The crowd is thinning," she said. "Fill a plate and join your friends if you wish. Or join your father. He's eating with the Lundgrens. Tell him I'll be along soon."

Kristin nodded and slipped away from the serving table, but she didn't take a plate. She wasn't hungry. She'd never be hungry again. She wandered in the direction of the cemetery and found a cool place in the shade of one of the tall tombstones. Hugging her legs and resting her chin on her knees, Kristin waited for Jenny to come.

CHAPTER THIRTEEN

❖ ❖ ❖

SHE didn't have long to wait. Jenny flopped down on the grass beside Kristin, her short, striped shawl askew, and asked bluntly, "What happened? I thought you liked Johan."

"I *do* like him," Kristin said.

"Well, then?"

Kristin put her hands to her head, which had begun to ache. "This isn't Sweden. It's the United States. I should have the freedom to make my own choice, not have my father decide for me whom I should marry."

"There are lots of girls who would choose Johan if they had the chance. I can't understand why you wouldn't."

"I want to go to the city. I want to work for women's right to vote."

"Is it *that* important to you?"

"It's important, yes. But it's even more important to me to have my father respect the fact that in this country I can be independent. I want him to believe that I can think for myself and make my own decisions."

"So that's the reason you did what you did. You turned down Johan to teach your father a lesson."

"No! That's not true!"

As tears blurred Kristin's vision, Jenny pressed a clean handkerchief into her hand. "I'm sorry," Jenny said. "I didn't mean to make you cry. All this is none of my business, and I shouldn't have said anything. I just hate to see you make a mistake."

"It's all right," Kristin answered. "We're friends, aren't we?" She wiped her eyes and tried to smile. Jenny couldn't be right. She hadn't wanted to teach Pappa a lesson . . . or had she? No! She hadn't!

"Of course we're friends," Jenny said, "no matter what. That's really what I came here to tell you." She struggled to her feet and smoothed down her festival skirt and apron. "The band's tuning up again, and they're going to start the circle games for the people our age. Want to come?"

"Not yet," Kristin said. "You go on without me. Paul will be looking for you."

"Will you be all right?"

"Of course." Kristin attempted another smile. "I'll see you later."

She was glad when Jenny left and she could think about what her friend had said. How could Jenny have been so mistaken? She had no wish to punish her father or Johan or anyone.

Johan . . . she desperately needed to talk to Johan. It would be a long walk to his farm, but she didn't mind. His parents would be at the festival for the rest of the day, and he'd be alone, so she'd have a chance to try to make up for the hurt she'd caused him.

Kristin hurried through the group, the noise of the

band keeping her from having to do anything more than smile and nod at the people she passed. Her parents were so busy chatting with the Lindens and the Petersons that they hadn't seen her pass by. She had reached a bend in the road and was nearly out of sight of the group when she heard someone call her name. She whirled around to see Sigrid striding toward her.

"Where are you going?" Sigrid called. "Surely you aren't leaving already?"

What Kristin wanted to do concerned only Johan. "I need to get away for a little while," she answered.

Sigrid gave a wry smile. "You're suffering from public opinion," she said. "If only we could get such strong public opinion for women's suffrage, Congress would quickly change the law; but people are more interested in their neighbors' business than in what they could do to make the world a better place."

At the moment Kristin didn't want to talk about suffrage. Since Sigrid obviously knew what had happened, Kristin wished she'd tell her she had done the right thing and had made the right choice, but instead Sigrid pulled a folded sheet of paper from the drawstring bag she carried and said, "The date is set. Anna Shaw will speak in one of the university auditoriums on Thursday, July tenth. I hope you and your mother will come and hear her. Remember, you have an invitation to stay with me."

Kristin took the flier from Sigrid, but she didn't look at it. Disappointment was a dull ache in her chest as she said, "We won't be able to go. It's hard making ends meet right now, and there isn't enough money to spend for train fare."

Sigrid smiled. "There's no problem with the transportation. You can ride with my sister and brother-in-law. On

113

July ninth they're taking a wagonload of handmade quilts to Minneapolis to exhibit at an arts fair and will return home on July twelfth. Fortunately the date for the fair coincides with the lecture, because I've insisted that Olga attend with me, and she actually agreed." She giggled and put a finger to her lips. "But Otto's not to know about it—until after they've arrived in Minneapolis!"

Kristin began to feel hopeful. If she could get Mamma to agree . . . "Thank you," she said. "I'll let Fru Dalquist know if I—we can go."

"Tell her in plenty of time," Sigrid said. "Forty miles is a long ride. They may spend the night halfway there, but in any case they'll leave before sunup."

"Thank you," Kristin repeated. She folded the flier once again and tucked it into a deep pocket in her skirt.

"I won't keep you," Sigrid said. "I want to get back in time to enjoy the maypole dancers."

Kristin watched Sigrid return to the Midsommarfest before she resumed her walk down the road.

She knew the way, but she had not been to the Olsens' farm before, and the walk was longer and hotter than she had imagined. Kristin had been sure she'd find Johan, so she felt lost when there was no answer at the house and Johan wasn't in the barn. She shouted his name, but he didn't answer.

It occurred to Kristin that he might not want to see her, but it didn't really matter now. The place had an empty feel to it. Johan wasn't there.

As Kristin sat on the edge of the well and tried to think of where he might be, a picture popped into her mind of Johan with his fishing pole. Of course. He was at the lake.

She followed a footpath that led into the woods and

down to the lakeshore and continued along it until she spotted him sitting silently on a rock, the pole propped in the ground and the line hanging limp in the water.

"Johan," Kristin called as she stepped through the trees to the small rocky cove, "will you let me talk to you?"

At the sound of her voice he glanced up, startled, but Kristin saw him pull into himself as he turned his face away from her. "In this country you have the freedom to say whatever you want," he said.

Kristin climbed up beside him on the rock. "Please don't be angry," she told him. "I came to apologize for being so rude and thoughtless Friday evening. I was so surprised at what our fathers had arranged, I spoke without thinking. I didn't mean to hurt you."

"What difference does it make?" Johan asked. "No matter how much you had thought about the offer of marriage, you still would have rejected it, wouldn't you?"

"I would have had to."

He shrugged as though her answer settled the question, but Kristin had more to say. "I rejected our fathers' arrangement. I didn't reject *you*."

"It's the same thing."

"No, it isn't."

"It is."

Kristin, perched close to Johan, laid the palm of one hand against his cheek and turned his head so that he had to look at her. "Listen to me. Look at me," she said.

His eyes were so dark and unhappy, Kristin wanted to throw her arms around him, hold him tightly, and comfort him, but slowly and calmly she said, "Which is better, to have a father say 'My daughter will marry you,' or to have the daughter say 'I want to marry you'?"

115

"Don't be ridiculous," he said. "That's not the way it's done."

Johan turned his head away, but with determination Kristin pulled it back. She was aware of the warmth of his skin under her hand, the line of his jaw, the strength in his face; and her fingers trembled. Jenny was right. There were many girls who would be eager to be married to Johan—and for good reason.

"I've known you only a short time, but I like you very much," Kristin said. "Someday that *like* could turn into *love,* and I'd come to you and say, 'Johan, I love you.' " The words, spoken aloud, seemed so natural, so real, that Kristin drew in a sharp breath of surprise.

Johan's eyes widened, and she could feel the muscles tense in his cheek. "Kristin, this is how I feel about you. This is why I was eager to have the prenuptial agreement."

"Forget the agreement," Kristin insisted. "That was something between our fathers. Liking, loving . . . that's something between you and me, just the two of us."

He moved so that he was facing her, and she could feel the warm pressure of his thigh against hers. "Do you think that love will come to us?"

Johan was wonderful, so kind and good . . . and exciting. Kristin rested her hands on his shoulders and looked into the depths of his eyes. "Yes," she said. "I think someday it will."

His face was close to hers, his mouth too tempting to resist. Kristin leaned forward and kissed him.

He wrapped his arms around her, and she drifted into the warmth of his lips and the salty, earthy fragrance of his skin.

Suddenly Johan pulled away and gripped her shoulders,

holding her at arm's length. With shock in his eyes he mumbled, "Kristin! I apologize. I have no right to endanger your reputation!"

Kristin smiled. "You didn't endanger my reputation. Remember, *I* kissed *you,*" she said, "and don't look so upset. It's the first time I've ever kissed a man."

"Kisses are supposed to be only for those who are married, or at least engaged."

"Haven't you ever been to a cornhusking bee? If a boy finds a red ear of corn, it gives him the right to kiss the girl who's his partner."

"A light kiss on the cheek? That's different."

"There was nothing wrong with our kiss, Johan. It was just my way of showing that I care about you."

"I care about you, too," he admitted. She could feel his muscles relax, and finally he smiled. "I've never kissed like that."

"Did you like it?" she teased.

"Of course I did."

"Then let's have our own, private, agreement—a kiss now and then, when we want to show each other that we care."

Johan's answer was in his eyes. Kristin lifted her face and kissed him again.

CHAPTER FOURTEEN

❖ ❖ ❖

THE day after Midsommarfest Pappa left on a short hauling job, and again the workload for Kristin and her mother doubled. Johan did not show up to help, which didn't surprise Kristin, even though they had parted on the friendliest of terms. What did surprise her was how much she missed him.

When Pappa returned, Mamma perked up. She was obviously more comfortable when he was home, and even the *spöken* she blamed for their troubles seemed less threatening to her.

The Fourth of July, which Kristin had heard was one of the United States' biggest holidays, passed without celebration in the community, although Pastor Holcomb spoke eloquently on the following Sunday about America's fight for independence.

Independence for whom? Kristin wondered. *How could people fight for independence but leave women out?*

The Young People's Society didn't meet during the

119

summer months, and the group meals after church services were curtailed because of the heat, so Kristin had little time in which to chat with Jenny. As far as all the other girls were concerned, what did it matter? They had made it clear they didn't approve of her behavior, but that was their problem, not Kristin's.

Johan attended church with his family, and Kristin was very much aware of his presence on the opposite side of the aisle. She tried to catch his eye, but when she realized that others were watching her, she blushed and stared straight ahead, refusing to allow herself so much as a glance in his direction. It was hard for Kristin to keep her mind on the service and at the same time battle the unfamiliar aching emptiness in her chest.

After the service Johan's family and hers hurried in opposite directions, so she had no chance to speak with him, and it was not long before the Swensens left the gathering and headed for home.

Kristin immediately ran up the stairs to her room. She had no sooner removed her cap, folded it, and placed it in the top drawer of the chest than her mother tapped lightly at the door, calling, "Kristin, may I come in?"

Hurrying to open the door, Kristin said, "Mamma, I'm coming right down. I'll help make dinner in a—"

Mamma gently shook her head and took Kristin's hand, leading her to a seat on the bed. "It's time to talk," she said.

"About what?"

"About you and Johan. I saw the way you looked at him in church. I saw how uncomfortable and unhappy you were, squirming away like a child kept after school."

"Mamma!" Kristin was shocked. "I wasn't squirming. I sat very still and kept my eyes on our pastor."

Mamma nodded. "Perhaps others couldn't see how you felt, but I could. I'm your mother."

Kristin looked away and didn't answer.

After waiting patiently for a moment Mamma said, "I think no matter how you behaved or what you said, you *do* care for Johan."

Furious because she felt her face flushing red, giving her true feelings away, Kristin murmured, "It doesn't matter."

"It matters more than you think, because it concerns your future."

Kristin pulled her hand from her mother's. "Please, Mamma, I don't want to talk about Johan, and my future is something I have to be responsible for myself—not you and not Pappa—just me."

Kristin cringed at the sorrow she heard in her mother's voice. "I thought perhaps you had reconsidered. It's obvious to me that you miss him."

"Yes, I do miss him." Kristin angrily rubbed at a tear that slid down her cheek. "But I don't regret what I did, and I don't want to talk about Johan anymore. Please!"

"Very well, Kristin," Mamma answered. She left the room, quietly shutting the door.

In the bottom of the chest in her room Kristin had hidden the folded paper that told about Anna Shaw's lecture. If Pappa came across it, he'd be sure to object. Kristin's only chance to attend the lecture was to approach Mamma. Knowing that Fru Dalquist would be attending might be reassuring to Mamma, and she in turn could influence Pappa. As each day passed, bringing her closer to July tenth, Kristin became more determined to go to Minneapolis.

121

She had worked out a plan. She'd be gone for at least three days—maybe four—but that was a short time, and Pappa could do her chores for her, couldn't he? It was only fair. She'd been doing most of his chores each time he worked away from home. Nervous about approaching her parents, knowing that each word would be crucial and she couldn't dare make a mistake, Kristin kept postponing the first step, her discussion of the lecture with Mamma.

On the morning of July seventh Kristin knew she could wait no longer. The moment Pappa left the house, heading for the barn, Kristin carried the dirty breakfast dishes to the sink for washing and asked, "Mamma, before we begin our chores, could we talk about something very important?"

A sudden spark of hope flashed in her mother's eyes. "Have you changed your mind about Johan? Do you want to talk about him?"

Kristin sighed. "This is not about Johan. I like him very much. Maybe even more than very much," she said, "but I want to talk about something else. Please sit down, Mamma. This is important to me."

Warily Mamma settled back into her kitchen chair and waited.

Kristin dropped into a chair opposite her mother and smoothed out the flier, placing it on the table. After a couple of hoarse attempts to speak, she was finally able to say, "The Dalquists are going to Minneapolis tomorrow. They're taking a wagonload of quilts to an arts fair."

"What does that have to do with us?" Mamma looked puzzled.

Kristin took a deep breath and let the story spill out. "The next evening a woman named Anna Shaw is coming to Minneapolis to speak about women's right to vote. Fru Dalquist is going to the lecture, and I—we've been invited, too."

"Fru Dalquist's sister is Fröken Larson. I can understand her attending the lecture to please her sister, but I can't understand her expecting you to go with her. She knows your help is needed at home."

Kristin shook her head. "Fru Dalquist doesn't even know I want to go."

"Well, then . . ." Mamma began to get to her feet, but Kristin reached out and clasped one of her hands.

"Please, Mamma, listen to me. I want very much to hear what Anna Shaw has to say. The fight for votes for women is a part of America. It's a part of my life."

"It is *not* a part of your life," Mamma said. "Your life is bound with the lives of your parents. We are a family. We came to America together, and we are working to establish a successful farm together. When you are older, your life will branch out from ours, but not now."

"It's only for three or four days," Kristin pleaded. "I'll be with the Dalquists on the journey, and I'll stay with Fröken Larson while I'm in Minneapolis."

"Your father will never agree."

"You could tell him it would be all right," Kristin said. "He'd listen to *you*."

They heard deep voices calling to each other outside the house, and Mamma jumped to her feet. "Someone is here," she said. She whipped off her apron and trotted to the front door, Kristin on her heels. They reached the parlor just as the door opened and Pappa stepped through.

"That was Herr Peterson with a message from the lum-

123

ber mill," he told them. "They need me to leave tomorrow on a delivery job that will take three days."

Sick with disappointment, Kristin saw her last chance disappearing. *Not tomorrow. No!*

Pappa held out two stamped and postmarked envelopes. "Herr Peterson also brought these. One is from your mother," he said as he handed a letter to Mamma. "And one is from your shipboard friend, Rebekah Levinsky," he told Kristin with a smile.

Kristin couldn't return the smile. Woodenly she accepted the letter.

Mamma carefully ripped one end of her envelope and shook out her mother's letter. "Listen," she said, a quaver in her voice. "I'll read the letter to you." She did, right from the beginning, and as *Mormor* related all the small details of encounters with friends and relatives, Kristin could visualize the marketplace, with stalls set up on the square, the church socials with fiddle music and candlelight, her cozy home in Leksand, and the happy, uncomplicated childhood she had known there. She missed her grandmother so much, she could hardly bear it.

At the end of the letter, as she read the endearments and the special message of love *Mormor* had sent to Kristin, Mamma's voice broke with a sob.

No one spoke. Pappa simply put a hand on Mamma's shoulder as though to lend his strength. Kristin, clutching Rebekah's letter to her chest, slowly climbed the stairs to her bedroom. She sat on the neatly made bed for at least five minutes, staring at the letter she'd been so eager to receive, unable to open it.

"Kristin?" Mamma called.

"Just a minute!" Kristin shouted back. If she were

going to read the letter from Rebekah, she had better stop daydreaming and do it now.

Tiny handwriting covered both sides of the sheet of paper as Rebekah brought Kristin up-to-date on family news, then told her about classes offered at the Hebrew Immigrant Aid Society center in New York City.

Someday I want to attend Columbia University. Who knows? I may even teach there! I can tell you this, Kristin, because I know you won't laugh at my dream. I'll always remember that you promised me I could make my wish come true in America, and I'm counting on that promise.

Kristin folded the letter and placed it back in the envelope. How well she remembered that promise she had made to Rebekah and Rose. Maybe Rebekah could fulfill her dream. Perhaps Rose could, too. But Kristin was being kept from realizing her own dream, and there was little or nothing she could do about it.

Pappa's voice thundered from the foot of the stairs. "Kristin! Come down here this minute!"

Kristin clattered down the stairs, startled by the anger in Pappa's voice. He waited for her, waving the flier she had left on the kitchen table.

"Your mother tells me you want to go to Minneapolis and hear this woman's lecture."

Kristin gulped. "Y-yes," she answered.

"What has come over you, Kristin? Your foolish ideas and actions have already caused great damage to you and to us, as well as to others."

What is the matter with my parents? Kristin thought

bitterly. *Don't my dreams mean anything to them?* "Why should I care what the people who live in Great Rock Lake think of me?" she exploded.

"You should care because in any community it's important for neighbors to live together in harmony."

"The only way the people around here want to live is the way they lived in Sweden!" Kristin complained.

Pappa's features hardened and he said, "We will have no more discussion about this lecture."

"But, Pappa, you don't understand."

"I understand enough to tell you that you cannot go to Minneapolis to hear this ... this idiotic discussion about women voting. I forbid it!"

"Pappa!" Kristin wailed, but he had turned his back on her, and there was no use at all in trying to plead with him.

In despair Kristin dropped to the bottom stair and hunched over, her head on her arms. Tears didn't come. She was far too angry to cry. How could Pappa decide who she was to marry, what she was to read, and where she was to go? The United States was a land of freedom, wasn't it? Shouldn't she have a right to that freedom, too?

CHAPTER FIFTEEN

❖ ❖ ❖

DURING the day, as Kristin went from one task to the next, she made plans. Pappa would be away on his job, so he wouldn't be on hand to stop her if she left for Minneapolis. However, if she did leave, then Mamma would be alone for three or four days and have the care of the animals as well as the house. Kristin pushed away the uncomfortable lump that tightened her throat. The task wasn't impossible, she told herself. Mamma could handle it.

Pappa left as soon as the cows had been milked and led to pasture. He entreated Kristin, "You mother needs you. I'm counting on your help."

"Don't worry about me. I'll be fine," Mamma told him.

"We'll both be fine," Kristin murmured, but didn't meet his eyes.

Diligently she weeded the kitchen garden and the potato field, swinging her hoe with sure, deft strokes. The chamber pots gleamed by the time she was through washing them, and the privy got an extra scrubbing. Kristin hated leaving the daily mucking out of the barn to Mamma, but there was no way she could do this chore in advance any more than the chores of milking the cows and feeding the animals.

But if the house was in perfect order, then there'd be little Mamma would have to do to it. Kristin swept and polished and overfilled the wood box next to the stove. She cleaned out the ashes, fed them to the garden, and worked on the stove until it shone.

She stopped only to join Mamma for the noon meal, but she ate quickly, eager to finish the list of jobs she had given herself.

Mamma, who had only picked at her food, leaned back in her chair. "Hard work is often a good way to get rid of unhappy feelings," Mamma said.

For the first time Kristin looked at her mother, whose hair was damp around her forehead and whose face was flushed.

She's been working hard, too, Kristin thought.

"There's a great deal I want to get done," Kristin answered. "By the time I finish, the house will be spotless. No heavy cleaning will have to be done to it for at least a week."

"Thank you," Mamma said. "I appreciate your help." A slight smiled wobbled across her lips, and she added, "You're a good girl, Kristin."

Kristin took a last bite, cleaning her plate, and answered, "Not many people would agree with you. They make it clear they don't like what I do."

"Sometimes I don't like what you do either," Mamma said, "but that doesn't mean you aren't a good girl.

Whether we agree on everything or not, you will always be my very dear daughter."

Feeling guilty, Kristin pushed back her chair. "I'll wash the dishes," she said. "You look tired, Mamma. Why don't you lie down for a while and rest?"

She was surprised when her mother answered, "Yes. I'll rest awhile. That's a good idea."

Kristin cleaned the kitchen, checked the pot of soup simmering on the back of the stove, and returned to work. Late in the afternoon—surprisingly late—she heard her mother come downstairs, so Kristin hurried upstairs, tugged a small travel bag from the storage room, and packed it with everything she'd need for her three-day trip.

She had no choice but to leave as soon as Mamma had fallen asleep. It was a long walk to the Dalquists' home, and Kristin needed to arrive before they began their very early morning journey. It would be awkward and noisy to go down the stairs in the dark with a travel bag; Kristin would have to hide it behind the chair next to the front door. Then, as she left the house, she could easily snatch up the bag and slip out without Mamma hearing her.

As Kristin crept down the stairs, clutching the travel bag, she paused now and then, listening intently. Mamma would be in the kitchen, adding to the soup and mixing the dough for tomorrow's bread. Mamma would understand why Kristin had to go . . . maybe not right away, but someday, when she had voted for herself, she'd surely understand.

Kristin tiptoed into the parlor and made directly for the chair by the door, but a light cough behind her startled her, and she almost dropped the bag.

She whirled around to discover Mamma seated in the chair by the window. In the dim light her face seemed dark and drawn.

"Don't defy your father, Kristin," Mamma whispered. "Please don't go."

"Why should Pappa control my life?" Kristin cried.

"Your father is working very hard so that we can have a good life here."

"We *had* a good life—in Sweden!"

Mamma sighed. "You know how it was in Sweden, Kristin. Your father was not a first son, so he did not inherit land. He worked long hours to buy every foot of land he owned. With the rise in taxes, the expense of living—our small farm could not have grown. Here in America we have the chance to develop a large and prosperous farm and become part of a thriving community. Can't you understand how much this means to your father?"

Put like this, Kristin did understand, and she wondered why neither Mamma nor Pappa had tried to explain it to her before. Resentfully she said, "Pappa could have talked to me. He could have taken the time to help me know why he had made these decisions, not just said 'Now we are going to America,' and 'Now we are buying the property *I* have chosen,' and 'Now *I* have decided who you are going to marry and when.' " A sob escaped as she added, "Pappa hasn't even tried to understand what I want to do. All he's said is 'I forbid it!' "

For a moment Mamma closed her eyes and held a hand to her forehead. "When you are grown," Mamma said, "you can fight for any cause you like. But now you are still our child, under our care, and we—" Her voice broke as she began to cough.

Kristin put down her bag and quickly lit one of the parlor lamps. In the stronger light she could see the beads of sweat on Mamma's forehead. She snatched up one of her mother's hands, and it was hot and damp. "Mamma! You're ill!" Kristin said. "Come with me. I'll help you up to bed."

Mamma resisted Kristin's efforts to pull her to her feet. "If you go . . ." she murmured.

"I'm not going anywhere. I'm staying here to take care of you," Kristin said firmly, although she wished she could sob loudly and kick her feet on the floor in frustration as she had done once as a child—only once, due to her mother's immediate action.

Mamma sagged, leaning against Kristin, who supported her up the stairs, one careful step at a time. "The *spöken* are not finished with us," Mamma mumbled, and she began to ramble about the woman who had died in the house. "It is *her* home, filled with memories of her husband and children. It's not our home, and it never will be."

"Hush, Mamma," Kristin soothed. She helped her mother undress and put on her long-sleeved cotton nightgown. Mamma's fever—for surely that must have been what had caused her to look so flushed earlier in the day—had returned. Kristin repeatedly bathed her mother's face, neck, and feet in cool water until the fever began to subside. Then she brewed a peppermint tea and spoon-fed it to her mother.

Mamma sighed and said something that sounded like "Thank you," then closed her eyes. Kristin fluffed up her pillows, straightened the coverlet, and went downstairs to quickly gulp down a bowl of the soup.

There was no time to dwell on what had happened.

131

With only a dull ache in her mind Kristin automatically went about the rest of the day's chores. After taking a quick peek at her mother, who still slept soundly, Kristin herded the cows into the barn, fed them, milked them, and stored the milk in the cooler.

She spooned off some of the broth from the soup into a bowl and carried it upstairs. Her mother was stirring, so Kristin asked, "How are you feeling, Mamma?"

Mamma's eyelids fluttered as she tried to focus on Kristin. "You're still here," she murmured.

"I told you I'd stay with you," Kristin answered. "I promise I won't leave."

Mamma closed her eyes again, but Kristin sat on the edge of the bed and held out the bowl of broth. "Eat a little of this," she said. "It will make you feel stronger."

"It hurts to raise my head," Mamma said.

"I'll feed it to you," Kristin told her. She gently lifted spoonful after spoonful to her mother's lips until the bowl was empty.

She lightly rested a hand on her mother's forehead. "Your fever has gone," she said. "Are you warm enough? Do you need another quilt?"

"I'll get it," Mamma said, and struggled to sit up, but she fell back against the pillow, murmuring, "I'm dizzy."

"Stay in bed," Kristin told her. She unfolded a quilt from the chest in the corner and spread it over the bed. "If you want anything at all, call me, Mamma. Please?"

"I don't want to be a bother," Mamma protested.

Kristin took her mother's hand. "How many times have you cared for me when I was ill? Now it's my turn to take care of you."

"Thank you," Mamma whispered, and closed her eyes. Kristin thought Mamma had dozed off again, but as she picked up the kerosene lamp to extinguish the wick, Mamma cried, "Don't take the lamp!"

"The light will keep you awake. The best way for you to get better is to sleep."

"It will keep away the *spöken*," Mamma whispered. "Please, Kristin, don't take the light away. The *spöken* . . . I can't let them—"

"All right," Kristin said, eager to calm her mother. "I'll keep the lamp right here on the table by your bed. You won't have anything to fear from *spöken*."

Mamma closed her eyes, and after a comforting pat and a tuck of the quilt, Kristin went to her own room and prepared for bed. She kept the door open so that she could hear if her mother called, and climbed into bed, hugging her Dala-horse for comfort. All day long Kristin had worked harder than she had ever worked in her life and she was exhausted; but after she turned off her lamp, she continued to stare at the ceiling, so miserable with disappointment, she was unable to sleep.

Aware of every little creak and groan of the house as it cooled during the night, Kristin began to wonder if perhaps Mamma was right and there really were *spöken* haunting this house and the people in it. Something seemed to be making life more difficult than it need be.

At some time during the hours that followed, Kristin drifted into sleep, only to awaken to a scream and a crash.

CHAPTER SIXTEEN

❖ ❖ ❖

KRISTIN stumbled to her feet and ran to her mother's bedroom. The bed was empty. "Mamma?" Kristin shrieked. "Where are you?"

"Kristin! Help me!" Mamma's muffled voice came from the floor on the other side of the bed, and as Kristin scrambled to reach her mother, she saw to her horror that the lamp chimney lay broken, the burning kerosene splashed on the window curtains and floor. Flames had begun racing up the edge of the curtains and spreading to the wall.

With all her strength Kristin got a firm grip on her mother's shoulders and tugged her to her feet. As fast as she could, she half-carried, half-dragged her mother around the bed and to the doorway. The flames spread, each red-gold flash snatching at another piece of wall or ceiling.

The fire, which crackled behind her, suddenly circled to the doorway just as Kristin struggled through.

"Mamma!" she cried, "Mamma, try to walk!" But her mother was a deadweight in her arms.

As a red ball of flame swooshed like a gust of wind across the ceiling above her head, carrying with it a cloud of black, choking smoke, Kristin stumbled, falling and rolling with her mother down a half flight of stairs. "I'm sorry, Mamma. I'm sorry," Kristin cried, but there was no time to check for bruises.

Praying for strength, she crawled down the rest of the stairs and across the hallway, scuttling like a crab and dragging her mother with her until she reached the front door. Kristin managed to open it and roll outside with her mother in her arms as the entering gust of air sucked a roaring spurt of fire and smoke over her head.

While flames curled up the side of the house, Kristin dragged her mother to safety far from the fire. She ran to the barn and loosened the cows.

Sparks! Kristin thought. *Sparks are carried by the wind! What if sparks land on the roof of the barn?* Frantically she ran to the pump, knocking over the bucket in her haste to fill it, and she cried aloud.

Suddenly Kristin was roughly pushed aside, and a man's voice shouted, "Where is your father?"

"He's not at home."

"Then tend to your mother. We'll take care of the barn. Are the animals out?"

"Yes," Kristin said. It was Herr Olsen, and beyond him was Johan, already climbing to the roof of the barn with a burlap sack, ready to beat out flying sparks.

Kristin raced around the burning house to the sheltered spot where she had left her mother.

Mamma was conscious now, and she clung to Kristin

as she knelt beside her. "Kristin, what is happening? Is this a bad dream?"

"No, Mamma." Kristin settled beside her mother and pillowed Mamma's head in her lap. "Our house is burning."

Bewildered, Mamma murmured, "How? Why?"

"I don't know. Your kerosene lamp fell, and there was no way to put out the fire. It spread so quickly, we barely got out of the house in time."

Mamma gripped Kristin's hand again and held it tightly. "You carried me out?"

Kristin patted her mother's shoulder. "We had a few bumps, and I had to drag you the last few yards. Are you hurting anywhere, Mamma? If you are, I'm sorry."

"You didn't hurt me," her mother said, and her fingers tightened on Kristin's hand. "You saved my life."

Silently, as Kristin and her mother watched the house turn to blackened, glowing chunks of charcoal chewed ragged by the flames, Kristin could feel tears rolling down her cheeks.

"There is nothing left," Mamma said.

"Not even a quilt I could wrap you in," Kristin answered.

"My photographs," Mamma said. "The beautiful wall hanging you made . . . all our treasures . . . they're gone."

With an empty ache in her chest Kristin murmured, "And the little Dala-horse *Mormor* gave me."

"There is no way the lamp could have fallen by itself," Mamma said.

"Did you reach for it? Did you try to get up?"

"No. I was asleep."

"But you were out of bed when I ran into the room," Kristin said. "You were lying on the floor."

"Not of my own will," Mama said firmly. "I know what I know. The *spöken* have done this. The woman who wanted us out of her house . . . she did her work well."

There was a sound of horses' hooves and wagon wheels bumping over the road, and Fru Olsen came into view. She jumped from her wagon, fastened the horses' reins to the fence, snatched up an armful of quilts, and ran as fast as she could to where Kristin was seated.

"Wrap up in this!" she shouted. "You will catch a chill wearing nothing but your nightdress in this night air! Where is your mother?"

"Here," Kristin said. "Mamma's ill."

"Then this is no place for her to be. Help me get her into the wagon. I'll drive you to our home and put the two of you to bed."

"I should stay here and help," Kristin protested, but Fru Olsen frowned.

"Nonsense. What can a young girl in a nightdress do to help? You'll do more good to stay out of the way. Let the men take care of things."

Another wagon arrived. Two men ran past saying, "We saw the flames. Is the family all right?"

"They're all right," Fru Olsen shouted. "My men are here somewhere—probably at the barn." She took Kristin's hand and pulled her to her feet. "Help me lift your mother," she ordered, and Kristin hurried to obey.

She sat in the back of the wagon, her mother's head again on her lap. Mamma's face was no longer hot and feverish, and she drifted into a troubled sleep, sometimes moaning as a wagon wheel dropped into a rut in the road and sometimes murmuring, "Linnart? Linnart?"

There was no way to find Pappa and bring him home,

Kristin knew. At least Herr Peterson might be able to make contact with Pappa when he reached his destination and let him know about the fire. Poor Pappa, Kristin thought. He'd had a dream, too, and just see what had happened to it. She longed to comfort him. With all her heart she wished he were on hand to comfort Mamma.

"Linnart?" Mamma murmured.

Kristin stroked her arm as she said, "It's all right, Mamma. Don't worry. Pappa will be here soon."

It didn't take long to reach the Olsens' home. With a flurry of activity the two middle Olsen boys were routed out of their beds, sheets were changed, and Mamma was tucked under a puffy quilt.

Fru Olsen tended Mamma carefully, finally drawing Kristin aside and saying, "Her lungs sound good, and she has no fever. There's a doctor in Scandia. We'll send for him tomorrow if necessary, but I think by then your mother will be much improved."

"Thank you," Kristin said. "You have done so much for us, and we are so grateful."

"We're glad to help. We're neighbors," Fru Olsen said bluntly. "Now, you take that other bed and go to sleep, Kristin. You've had a frightening experience, and the best cure for that is rest."

"There must be something I can do to help."

"Well . . ." Fru Olsen said, "you need your sleep, but tell me first, how did the fire happen? Where did it start?"

Kristin poured out the story, reliving it for the first time, even telling Fru Olsen that Mamma blamed the *spöken*, hoping that this kind woman would help to put Mamma's mind at rest.

But to Kristin's surprise Fru Olsen nodded. "Ever since

the tragedy in that house there has been a bad feeling about it."

"You believe in *spöken*, too?"

"Who knows what is out there? We have all heard many strange stories from people who had only the truth to tell. You young people are too quick to dismiss things you can't see or understand." She gave Kristin a friendly pat on the shoulder and said, "I have selfishly kept you up too long. Climb into bed and I'll turn out the lamp."

The minute Kristin had pulled the quilt up around her ears, she dropped into an exhausted slumber filled with strange dreams. She was chasing a transparent woman, flames shooting from her hair and fingers, and all the while the woman was crying, "Out of my house! Get out! Get out!" As the lake rose up to smother the flames, the woman rode off on Kristin's little Dala-horse.

"I want my horse! Give it back!" Kristin cried.

"Never mind, Kristin," she heard her mother saying. "Maybe your grandmother can send you another."

Kristin felt a hand softly stroking her forehead and woke to see her mother seated at the side of her bed. Sunlight flooded the room, touching Mamma's hair with gold.

"Mamma," Kristin cried as she struggled to sit up. "I was dreaming . . . I . . ." As she realized where she was and what had happened, she cupped her mother's face between her hands and studied it. "How are you feeling?" she asked. "You were so ill that you fainted."

"I'm much better," Mamma said. "I'm still a little weak, but the worst has passed." Suddenly her face crumpled, and she reached forward, holding Kristin tightly. "We've lost everything, Kristin."

"No, we haven't, Mamma," Kristin said, and tried to

sound encouraging. "Pappa has his land and the animals, and we can work to build another house."

"That's true," Mamma said, and she sat back, wiping tears from her eyes with the back of one hand. "But think of all the possessions we've lost. How will we get enough money to replace the food and clothing and furniture?"

"Maybe I can get a paying job," Kristin said. "Perhaps the Lundgrens need help in their store, or the milliner in her shop. There must be something."

Mamma shivered, so Kristin quickly led her back to her own bed and tucked her in. "I'll get dressed and go downstairs to make you some tea," she said, then stopped, putting her hands to her face. "I can't wander around in my nightgown," she said. "What am I going to wear?"

The door suddenly opened, and Anna, the six-year-old Olsen girl, stood there. "I'm supposed to tell Mamma when you wake up," she said. "And I'm not to come in without knocking. Oh. I forgot."

"It's all right," Kristin told her, and smiled reassuringly. "Thank you, Anna."

The child disappeared, and in just a few moments Fru Olsen knocked at the bedroom door.

Kristin opened the door, and Fru Olsen bustled in, a pile of clothing over one arm, a steaming cup of tea in her other hand. She looked at Mamma with a sigh of relief. "I'm glad to see you are much improved over last night. I was prepared to send for the doctor."

With a quick gesture to Kristin to prop her mother up with pillows, Fru Olsen handed Mamma the cup of tea. She then held out the clothes to Kristin. "Fru Berglund sent some of these to you, and some are from Fru Linden and Fru Nelson. You know their daughters, I think—Esther and Josie."

"They know about the fire already?"

"Of course. The women of Great Rock Lake are gathering together quilts, dishes, clothing—everything you'll need to replace what you've lost. The men are clearing the land for the house raising."

"The what?" Mamma cried. Kristin was speechless.

"When the land is cleared," Fru Olsen said, "the men will get together and build you a new house. The women of course will bring food. It will be quite a party."

"They would do all this for us, even though we've been here such a short time?" Mamma asked.

"And in spite of disliking me?" Kristin murmured.

Fru Olsen put an arm around Kristin's shoulders. "Kristin, dear," she said, "no one dislikes you. We may not understand you, and we may disapprove of some of the things you do, but we know you're a good girl from good parents, and we like you—very much."

Kristin, immersed in guilt for her attitude toward the people in Great Rock Lake, was suddenly blinded by tears, but Fru Olsen didn't allow her a minute of remorse. "Hurry and dress," she said. "You offered your help, and, among other things, I need you to watch the younger children. Tilde is being even more naughty than usual and needs some extra attention. There's a hairbrush and mirror for your use on the dresser."

With no time to think, Kristin dressed, brushed and braided her hair, took her mother's empty teacup, and trotted downstairs and out to the kitchen. Fru Olsen insisted on carrying a bowl of beef broth to Mamma, but she had prepared a hearty breakfast for Kristin.

Kristin ate quickly, washed the dishes that were still in

a pan on the drainboard of the sink, and tidied the kitchen, even sweeping the back porch. Tilde, who had been pulling on her skirts, wanted to go outside, so Kristin shepherded Tilde and Anna through the back door.

Because the kitchen garden needed weeding, Kristin made a game of it, and even Tilde, who plucked a carrot or two by mistake, joined in the fun. Kristin let her pick a few more and brought them into the kitchen, washing them and leaving them in a neat pile on the drainboard.

Fru Olsen was pleased when she saw what Kristin had done, and she didn't hesitate to give her other tasks to do. "When my girls are old enough, it will be such a pleasure to have them work beside me as you are doing," she said.

"Maybe the boys would also like a chance to work beside you," Kristin said. "I saw rhubarb in your garden, and I know where I can find wild strawberries. I'm still learning how to bake, but I know enough to be able to teach Arnold and Carl to bake a pie."

Fru Olsen broke into laughter. "That's a good joke. Can you imagine a man setting foot inside a kitchen, except to carry in wood or enjoy eating what has been cooked?" She handed Kristin utensils and napkins to set around the table and busied herself putting finishing touches on the noon meal.

"Why shouldn't a man be able to bake a pie? I'd be glad to let Kristin teach me."

Kristin whirled to see Johan standing in the doorway, his hair in wet ringlets around his face, his neck and arms still damp from his washing up in the basin outside the door.

"You're early, son," Fru Olsen said, and began firing off questions, not waiting for answers. "Find a wooden box—a large one—and help me wrap up some of this food. Are there many men on hand to help? Will this be enough, do you think? Here . . . put in an extra loaf of bread."

Johan had time only to wink at Kristin before his mother had filled his arms and shooed him out the door. Had Johan been teasing?

The kitchen was hot, and Kristin brushed an arm across her sweaty forehead. For that matter, why *couldn't* women have the opportunity to cool off in the lake?

Kristin took a plate of food upstairs to Mamma, who had just awakened from a morning nap and was gaining color in her cheeks. She chatted with Mamma, telling her what she'd been doing, then hurried back to the kitchen to join the others.

Carl and Arnold sneaked grinning looks at Kristin and tried to snatch buttered noodles from each other's plate. Anna spilled her milk, and Tilde kept trying to climb out of her chair and into Kristin's lap, until her mother tied her in place with a dish towel across her chest and under her arms.

As though she knew Kristin would have questions, Fru Olsen said, "It will take a few days to clear and level the land. Did I tell you that they were able to save the barn?"

"What can we possibly do to repay all of you?" Kristin asked.

"The next time someone else in the community needs help, you can step in and give it," Fru Olsen answered. "That's the only way to repay what is given to you."

Kristin stroked the skirt of the pretty blue cotton dress she was wearing. "All this wonderful generosity—repayment would take a lifetime."

But I don't plan to be here for a lifetime, Kristin

144

thought just as Tilde dropped her bowl upside down in her lap and howled, ending the conversation.

While Fru Olsen cleaned up her youngest child and carried her upstairs for her nap, Kristin sent the boys out to fetch wood for the stove and handed Anna a clean dish towel. The dishes were soon washed, and Anna was allowed to play.

When Fru Olsen returned, Kristin told her to rest. "But show me first where you keep the yeast and the flour," she said. "I'll be glad to set a batch of bread dough to rise."

"What a good girl you are! I would love the help!" Fru Olsen said. Her eyes sparkled. "But before you start with mixing the dough, there is a guest waiting to see you in the parlor."

"A guest?"

"And she has a gift for you. Go and see."

Kristin hurried to the parlor—a duplicate of every Swedish parlor—and stopped at the door. "Jenny!" she exclaimed as she saw her friend waiting for her.

"Oh, Kristin!" Jenny cried, and ran to hug her. "I'm so sorry about your house!"

"It's hard to believe it happened," Kristin said. "This morning I thought it was only a terrible dream."

Jenny reached into the pocket of her skirt and slowly brought forth a bright red Dala-horse. "I brought you a gift," she said.

"Your horse?" As Jenny nodded, Kristin cried, "Oh, Jenny, I couldn't take it!"

"It didn't come from your grandmother, but it will remind you of her," Jenny said. "Please, Kristin. I want to give it to you."

As Kristin took the little horse and clutched it to her

chest, mourning the Dala-horse her grandmother had given her, she realized that for everyone there is always a tugging in the heart for home. Sigrid ... Johan ... Mamma, in her own way ... how many people had tried to tell Kristin that change must come in its own time.

But eventually it will come, Kristin thought, and she bent her head to hide her tears.

Chapter Seventeen

❖ ❖ ❖

MAMMA was completely well by the day of the house raising. Entire families arrived at the Swensen property, beginning at sunup. While the men and older boys worked to frame the house, the women presented food in great quantities. Some formed circles in which they sewed and embroidered and even worked on a large hooked *ryamattor* for the floor of the Swensens' new parlor. Small children darted in and out underfoot, occasionally climbing the large piles of cut lumber—still fragrant with oils from the heart of the wood—heedless of shouts to get off and stay off.

As Pappa, with Herr Olsen at his side, took command, Kristin was amazed to see the force and vitality her father possessed. He had been stunned at news of the fire and badly shaken at the loss of all their possessions. But he had recovered, strengthened by the support of the neighbors in Great Rock Lake, and now he was like a young man, working with the others to hoist beams and nail supports in place, his hair glistening with sweat, his shirt plastered to his back.

Kristin could see him through her mother's eyes, much as Mamma must have seen him when they were both very young, and she understood more about two people needing each other and wanting to be together and sharing dreams.

No matter what chore she was assigned during the day, from washing drinking cups to watching the littlest children, Kristin found herself looking for Johan. And sometimes, to her delight, she discovered that his eyes were already on her.

Once he stopped, stepping back into the shade of a large elm tree in order to wipe his dripping face with a towel, and she hurried to bring him a cup of cool water. "I can't thank you enough for all you are doing for us," she told him.

Johan shook his head. "There's no need for thanks. This is something we all want to do." He smiled. "You'd do the same for any of us, wouldn't you?"

"Yes," Kristin said. "Johan . . ." She hesitated, and he waited for her to continue. Finally she took a deep breath and blurted out, "Johan, you are sweaty and dirty, and there's a streak of mud down one side of your face."

"Is that a compliment?"

Kristin took a step closer and dropped her voice. "No. I'm saying that in spite of all that, the way that I feel about you I wish I could kiss you right now."

Johan looked startled. "Kristin, there are people all around us."

"Don't worry. I won't do it. I just told you what I'd *like* to do." She glanced back and saw Fru Olsen watching her intently. When Fru Olsen's eyes met Kristin's, she smiled and turned away. Kristin said to Johan, "I think your mother likes me now."

"She always has."

"I mean, I think she'd be happy if we—"

"If we what, Kristin?"

Kristin's pulse quickened, and she found it hard to breathe. "Johan," she said, "independence means a great deal to me. I couldn't be happy in a country that promised freedom to all its citizens yet gave it to only some of them."

He nodded. "This is the way you are. I understand."

Kristin gulped and continued before she lost her courage. "You said you wouldn't stand in the way if I wanted to go to meetings in Minneapolis and work for women's right to vote."

"That's true."

"And you said it was because you'd respect my right to work for causes I believe in."

"Of course."

The sinking feeling in her stomach began to disappear, and she felt almost light-headed. "Would you really let me teach you how to bake a pie?"

He grinned. "Why not?" Cocking his head to one side, he studied her. "Does this mean that you'll be staying in Great Rock Lake?"

Kristin blushed. "The idea of living in a city is exciting, but that was before you . . . that is, before I . . . I can see that much of the work I want to do needs to be done here, too, and I'm glad because . . ." It was all Kristin could do to keep from throwing her arms around him. "Oh, Johan, this is hard for me to say, but when I am eighteen and you're twenty-one, will you marry me?"

"I don't know," he answered.

Kristin's smiled vanished. She suddenly felt frightened and cold, but Johan took her hands, and his voice was warm.

"You set certain conditions. I have conditions as well. I believe that marriage is a partnership, and a husband and wife should work together to make it a strong partnership, putting each other first."

Kristin thought of her own parents. "So do I," she answered quickly.

"And I believe that wives should be cherished, but husbands deserve to be cherished, too."

Kristin giggled. "We're still in agreement."

There was a long pause, and his eyes grew serious. "Now, this is even more important. You've made me believe that love given freely is necessary to a happy marriage. You said someday you'd tell me you love me. Do you love me, Kristin?" he asked.

Her heart pounding at the sound of the words, Kristin was sure of her feelings. "Yes," she whispered. "I love you."

With a mischievous light in his eyes Johan said formally, "Then, Kristin Swensen, since I love you, too, I accept your proposal of marriage. The next step is for your father to talk to my father."

Kristin burst into laughter, and Johan laughed with her. A few of the men working nearby turned to see what was happening and smiled at them indulgently before going back to their jobs.

"I've got to work," Johan told her. "But after your house is built, we can talk to our parents about our decision. We might even be in for another celebration."

Kristin, dangling the drinking cup from one finger, strolled back to where her mother was seated with a group of other women, all of them taking tiny, almost-invisible stitches in the narrow, rolled hems of large napkins. "Would you like me to help?" she asked as she sat with them.

Fru Berglund handed Kristin a large square of cloth and a threaded needle, and the women, with smiles and nods in Kristin's direction, resumed their conversation.

Kristin looked around at the people working to help them, and she felt such a rush of belonging, she could hardly contain her happiness. It seemed like such a long time ago that she had been angry and resentful about having to move to the United States, and now she was glad her family had come. Life wasn't going to be easy. There was a great deal of hard work ahead. But here in America she'd have the freedom to reach her dream.

The United States was a land in which there was more than one way of doing things and more than one person making decisions. It was a land in which more than one dream was possible. She smiled to think that because of her pact with Johan her parents' dreams could also come true.

One of the women in the group said to Mamma, "Fru Swensen, would you mind repeating the story of the *spöken* in your house? Olga Johnson hasn't heard it."

Before her mother could say a word, Kristin said, "Mamma, the *spöken* are gone with the old house. The new house is ours, and there'll be no *spöken* in it. In honor of chasing away any and all *spöken*, I'm going to paint a sign to hang over the front door. It's going to say *Welcome to the Happy Home of Linnart and Gerda Swensen*."

The women smiled, and Mamma said, "Don't forget to add *Kristin*. It's your home, too."

Hugging her secret happiness to herself, Kristin nodded agreement. Great Rock Lake—for a while with her parents and then with Johan—would be her home, but there would be trips to Minneapolis and Saint Paul, maybe even to Washington, D.C.

Kristin knew she had a great deal to learn about the work women had done in the United States to gain the right to vote and about the work still needed to be done, but when changes would be made, she—Kristin—would actually take part in them.

Be patient, she told herself, and smothered a giggle as she added, *Well, at least try to be.*

The day was glorious, Johan was wonderful, and the future was exciting. Even though it might be true that change sometimes came slowly, Kristin's dream was about to be realized, and she was ready.

ABOUT THE AUTHOR

JOAN LOWERY NIXON is the acclaimed author of more than ninety fiction and nonfiction books for children and young adults. She is a three-time winner of the Mystery Writers of America Edgar Award and the recipient of many Children's Choice Awards. Her popular books for young adults include *High Trail to Danger* and its companion novel, *A Deadly Promise*; the best-selling Orphan Train Quartet, for which she received two Golden Spur Awards; the Hollywood Daughters trilogy; and the first two books of the Ellis Island series, *Land of Hope* and *Land of Promise*.

Mrs. Nixon and her husband live in Houston, Texas.